AF415290

Invincible: A Western Novel

Richard G. Hole

Wild West

RESUME

Three outlaws, stationed in the rough terrain, suddenly appeared on the path, pointing at him.

But as soon as they had stopped the traveler and were trying to surround him to deprive him of the money, he, with the acquired lightness, took out the small revolver that he carried at his waist, and with two accurate shots, which vibrated almost simultaneously, he shot down two of the men. outlaws.

When the third, astonished, wanted to react and repel the aggression, a new shot brought him a hand and a revolver, forcing him to fall down an embankment so as not to suffer the fate of his companions.

Invincible is a story belonging to the Wild West collection, a collection of novels developed in the American Wild West.

INVINCIBLE

Bud Raines was born with the "Colt" in hand, according to the unanimous affirmation of all the inhabitants of the region. We do not dare to assure that materially this would have happened like this, but metaphorically, no one would have allowed to assure that it was not true.

The morning that he came into the world in a cheerful town next to one of the great bends that forms the Colorado River, called Grand Canyon, between the Indian reservations of Havasupai and little Colorado, his grandfather, old Kelly, affirmed very seriously when observing that Bud came to the planet fiercely biting both fists:

"Look at him, poor thing; He comes mad because he has not been able to go out shooting a good "Colt" of 45, like all his family.

And realizing that it was his duty to provide the newborn with so longed"for gadget, he took his out of its holster, stripped it of the bullets, and placed it in Bud's trembling hands, who angrily raised the barrel to his mouth as if it was the tastiest bottle.

Since that day, the favorite toy to silence him when he caught a dog was the revolver. Grandpa Kelly, turned into his governess, held it in his hands, clicking the trigger to distract the boy, and when Bud started walking, he found him an old revolver, tied a rope to the striker and Bud dragged him along. through the ranch rooms as if it were a vehicle bought in the most luxurious bazaar.

When Bud was eight years old, his grandfather insisted that the time had come to begin the neophyte's primary instruction, making him seriously rehearse the handling of the weapon. Old Kelly, a great taster of temperaments, claimed that his grandson's blood was a charge of dynamite with a lit fuse inside and, therefore, a man of such temperament had no more dilemma than to learn to handle the revolver better than anyone. or worrying about acquiring a good grave in the village cemetery, to occupy it the moment his blood warned him that he had ceased to be a boy to aspire to become a man.

And to faith that old Kelly was right. Long before he expected, Bud had a chance to show his impetuousness and to attest to how well he had put his grandfather's lessons to good use.

When he was only twelve years old, one day he went out with his father to make a trip to a nearby town called Apex, where his father had to collect the amount of some cattle sold.

They were returning to the Grand Canyon at dusk, when three outlaws, stationed in the rough terrain, suddenly appeared on the path, pointing at Bud's father and despising him for considering him a creature with the bottle still between his teeth; But as soon as they had stopped the traveler and were trying to surround him to deprive him of the money, Bud, with the lightness that his grandfather had made him acquire to handle the weapon, took out the small revolver that he carried at his waist, and with two accurate shots, that vibrated almost simultaneously, struck down two of the outlaws and when the third, astonished, wanted to react and repel the aggression, a new shot brought him a hand and a revolver, forcing him to fall down an embankment so as not to suffer the fate of his companions.

The feat spread by word of mouth throughout the region and Bud began to be regarded with respect, when he was only of an age to receive a spanking for his antics.

The strange thing was that Bud was not tragically thrilled by his feat. The blood did not seem to impress him and, when his grandfather forced him to repeat for the umpteenth time the details of his feat, the boy assured very formally:

"It was something precious, grandpa." He really wanted to rehearse on someone, because he was already tired of throwing the trees and wild ducks. It seems to me that the next time I shoot again, I will shoot on that brute Fred Sanders, who has made me bite the ground several times with his terrible fists.

Fred Sanders was the son of Bud's father's ranch foreman, a tall, stocky boy, the same age as Bud and Bud's best friend. Together they had grown up loose in the pastures, without fearing God or the devil, and together they had carried out countless small robberies typical of their age, helping each other when someone suffered a disaster.

The two loved each other like brothers; But when their differences of opinion exploded, they settled the criteria with their fists, and although Bud was strong and tough, his friend was more skillful and ended up beating him.

When this happened and Bud was angry, but without shedding a tear, bleeding from the mouth or nose, Fred would carry him on his shoulder, ignoring the kicking of his friend, transferring him to the nearest stream, washing his wounds with the care that I would do it with a little brother and then I would say to him:

"Well, Bud, don't hold a grudge against me." I do it like this so that you learn to defend yourself with fists, that fists also serve a purpose. Someday you will be able to me and that day you will have learned something that you will have to thank me for.

But Bud didn't learn to beat Fred. He had rehearsed his sturdy fists on other boys older than him, succeeding in applying them terribly; but when he relapsed with his friend, he was fatally defeated by him, and failure kindled his blood and he vowed to take fierce revenge upon him.

Grandpa Kelly, he saw himself and wanted to put that idea out of his mind. He should not do that with the best friend he owned, and if Fred was more skilled with his fists than he was, his obligation was to learn to handle them better, to defeat him nobly.

The success of that day was terrible for him. Emboldened by this display of mastery of the weapon, he did not shy away from showing off as a small gunman, and when the bozo began to point under his nose and he thought he was a man with the right to alternate between real men, he did so with such bragging that more than once he was forced to have to show that what he released through his tongue he could sustain with the gun in his hand.

Being eighteen years old, and very shortly before his father died, and a collapse occurred in his life that almost plunged him into tragedy, he heard people say from the valley that a terrible gunman called "el Rojo del Colorado ", and that he, using his fame and his safety handling the revolver, was fleecing all the industrialists of Gran Canyon, living like a king and forcing the gamblers to give him a bonus for every night they opened the game. in the gambling dens.

Bud didn't care if he ripped off the gamblers. He hated them, because he had the suspicion that on one occasion they had won him five hundred dollars with bad arts, although he could not verify it; but he could not admit that no one in the region presumed to command respect with weapons in hand while he was there, and he decided to finish off the bully.

He looked for Fred and simply proposed:

"Do you want us to go down to the village and finish off that boastful and conceited "Red"?

"Well; But, don't you think that two for one is going to be a bit cowardly?

"Not. We are going to propose one thing to you. We give you five minutes to ride a horse and get out of town. If I don't want to, then let him choose between you punching him, or me shooting. Maybe he despises you, but accepts me, and then ...

"Well, accepted." That you choose; But if it kills you, tell me I'll turn it into pulp later.

"Seem right. I'll do the same to him if he beats you first.

That night they appeared at "El Gallo Verde", where the bully stopped more frequently, and when they discovered him at a Pharaoh's table, watching the game, Bud approached him, dropped his hand on his shoulder and without further ado preambles he said:

"Listen, friend; This one " this was Fred " and me, it bothers us a lot that here, where we were born, there is no one who claims to be stronger and more skilled than us. They say that you boast of having iron fists and agility of hands, driving the "Co1t", that there is no one equal to you. Well, here we are ready to show you your mistake, and we don't give you to choose more than two paths: either you fight with his fists, or shoot me, or you have five minutes to leave town and forget about the route. where you can return to it.

The gun"man looked at them smiling, very amused, as he considered them two beardless boys, unconscious and boastful; but since the challenge had been formal and in front of many people he answered with irony:

"I am not used to spanking children, because I have never considered it a man's thing;" But when children insist on being spanked, they must be pleased. I'll give this fist"bragging brat a good beating first, and then I'll put two bullets in your ribs so you have to scratch for a while.

"Well, stay with the plan." Now, tell us if you prefer violets for your grave, or are you more fond of evergreens. We are in the habit of giving a crown to everyone to whom we provide eternal rest, and you will not be the exception.

The bandit burst out laughing and said:

"I don't want to ruin you guys." With a good bunch of thistles, I'll have plenty.

"Very well. Well, you will be pleased.

The crowd, who knew Bud and Fred well, were delighted by this event. Only that couple of madmen could free them without exposure, for their part, from the robberies of the gunman, and they awaited the fight with expectation, since they considered both worthy rivals.

Fred stripped off his leather jacket and waistcoat, rolling up the sleeves of his shirt to reveal two not very thick arms, but with terribly cultivated muscles, and addressing "the Red one", who was proceeding with the same operation. , He said:

"Anytime you want we can start the show."

They all stared at the outlaw's hairy, blackened arms, and deep down they didn't bet a dollar on Fred. His rival was much tougher and heavier, and they presumed that he was going to award him a beating to death.

The fight began in the game room of the gambling den, which had been cleared, leaving a great space for the contestants, and they, in a magnificent fight, began the fight that was tough, spectacular and exciting.

"El Rojo", despite his strength and his fists, received terrible caresses from Fred's, who fought with the utmost courage; but he also knew how to administer terrible blows to his rival that made his face look like a pity.

Both bled from the mouth, nose, and eyebrows, neither yielding in the terrible contest; but it was observed that Fred could withstand less than his resistant enemy and that if the combat was not null, it would lean in favor of the gunman.

So it was. When both were already exhausted, "the Red" managed to place, in an oversight, his enormous fist on the chin of his rival, and he, caught by surprise and with his energies turned off, rolled on the floor, leaving him senseless. .

The outlaw flopped down on a stool, huffing like a bear, and asking for whiskey to collect himself, and Bud, who was watching him calmly, came up to him, saying:

"I suppose you will not be in a good condition to handle the revolver and I don't want them to say that I take advantage of it to kill you like a chicken." I give him all night to rest and get well, and tomorrow, at ten o'clock, I'll come get him so we can finish this matter. I have made up my mind that after five past ten you should not cast a shadow over the land of this town, and I will not give you another minute.

The bandit, stressed by his triumph, accepted the truce and, after almost draining a bottle of whiskey, retired to rest.

Bud took the inanimate body of his friend and transferred it to the ranch, where he took care of resuscitating him, which cost him a lot of work, and when he succeeded, he said:

"You weren't bad, but your tactic was wrong." You should have worked his stomach instead of trying to break his teeth. I'm glad someone spanked you once in life, but I'm going to get back at you. Tomorrow I'll kill that braggart idiot and when you're hot, I'll give you a bigger beating than he ever gave you for letting you beat.

The next day, at the scheduled time, he went to "El Gallo Verde" in search of the gunman, who had come to the appointment like a real man. Fred had been obstinate in accompanying his friend, because if he fell like a ram, he was ready to fight again with the undesirable and paralyze his heart to beat to avenge his friend Bud.

He proposed:

"Let's go to a place where we don't dirty the floor with our filthy blood." Two hundred meters away there is a very good alfalfa field for them to bury us in it.

The bandit accepted and they went to the field. Already there, a cowboy was lent to act as godfather.

The contestants were placed at twelve meters, with their arms hanging along the body, and the judge withdrew warning that he would give a preventive slap and another to hurry to shoot.

Bud, serene as if attending a rodeo, had his eyes fixed on those of "Red", who did not seem very calm before the calm of that almost beardless boy, who seemed to have judged too lightly, and when vibrated the first slap, both stiffened with the ear attentive to the final.

When it vibrated like a cannon shot, Bud's right hand moved in an unlikely way. No one who attended the duel realized how he had reached the butt of the revolver and how he had fired; but the fact was that, when "Red" had half extracted from the holster his huge "Colt", he had received a shot in the middle of the heart that deprived him of finishing his attempt.

"The Red One" fell flat on the alfalfa, burying his face in it, and Bud calmly turned to Fred, saying:

"Let's see when you learn to shoot like that." You are an ass handling the "Col", and I think you are even moving your fists.

"Well," Fred said calmly. When I heal I will show it to you in your own flesh.

That afternoon the outlaw was buried, and Bud, complying with his offer, said a prayer for the dead man's soul and placed the bundle of thistles on his grave.

Despite this desire for a fight and blood, Bud was neither a hardened boy nor a sadist. He had a heart of gold and was splendid to satiety, and only when it came to the register of his self"esteem in handling the weapon, did he become a beast and did not recognize friends or enemies.

His exploits had caused him much displeasure, and the young man, realizing that the town was not a great experimentation field for his destructive skills, longed to get out of it and travel the West, in order, without hindrance or restriction, to put into effect his desire to Fight; but his father's opposition was fierce and Bud was forced to satisfy the author of his days, whom he loved madly.

But a little later, old Jim passed away unexpectedly, and Bud, instead of holstering the "Colt" and taking care of his estate, it occurred to him that this was the right time to please his friends. eagerness and, without prior consultation with anyone, he sold the ranch and decided to leave at random.

The day he was getting ready to fly, he looked for his faithful friend Fred and said:

"Well, wingless bird, here I am leaving you to rot between this valley and those calcareous walls of the Colorado." I'm going to run the world and give pleasure to the finger. I hope that when I return, if I return, your fists have not calloused from not using them anymore.

Fred angrily swore:

"Don't make fun of it, damn your figure! You take advantage to make fun, because you have money to afford that luxury and I don't. If I had the dollars you have in my pocket, you wouldn't tell me that.

Bud shook him by the shoulder, yelling:

"You dirty coyote! ... What are you saying? Is it just the money that binds you here? What do I have it for then? Do not disguise your cowardice with subterfuge. If what you say is true, pack your gear and follow me! As long as I have a dollar in my pocket, it will belong to both of us.

Fred did not make himself repeat the order. He went home, packed his luggage, fixed his horse, and that night, stealthily so as not to arouse the suspicions of his father, who had remained as foreman of Bud's ranch with its new owners, they set out west to enter California.

They were three wonderful years of wild and quarrelsome life in Utah, Nevada, Arizona and California. Spending the proceeds from the sale of the ranch, without any concern, they toured the hardest parts of the West, always among people who were rough and light"handed, and although they were in charge of many glorious and triumphal acts, more than once they served as a field experimentation for the old"fashioned local doctors, who tried new procedures for savage cures on them, without the devil being able to take to their dominions that famous pair of fighters who only fought for the pleasure of fighting and to keep their vanity as men taut skilled in fighting.

But one day, with many suffered emotions and a few ounces of lead inside their skin, they realized that money was coming to an end, and since they had satiated their desire for freedom and brawling, they studied the situation for the first time calmly and They decided that the best way was to return to the lost home.

Bud didn't realize that he no longer had a home in Grand Canyon. He had sold it and undercut it in those three years of wild life, and all he was going to find there were many memories, some pleasant and some painful, but nothing more.

Instead, Fred had his father. This had been forced to leave the position because of an accident suffered in a rodeo that injured his foot, but his employers had assigned him a small pension with which he could hardly live.

When they entered the town, the people had almost forgotten about them. Many cowboys were new and knew Bud only by name; Others had erased from their memory the exploits of the beardless Bud, now a hardened man, tough, more built and more attractive than when he left, and no one paid attention to the man who returned with the crown of the victor, although this crown was I would have worn out on the trip.

Fred's father welcomed them with open arms, forgiving the prodigal son's flight and, after the moment, went into inquiries about their plans.

"I come to work, Father," Fred said. There is nothing left for me to see in the West and you need my help. Find me a ranch and I will be a useful and tough pawn there.

"Very well, maybe I can get it." And you, Bud, what plan are you up to?

"May the devil take me if I know," said the waiter. I have come on impulse that I did not stop to examine. Now ... Of course, without money, I have no choice but to work.

"About what?

"What the hell is it going to be? Do I know anything other than handling cattle?

"I suppose not, but ... won't you feel denigrated working where you should be a true master?"

"To hell the pride of what you cannot have! I was what I was and I will be what I should be. I'll try to find a job as a foreman if they want to give it to me and they think I'm good for it and then ... God will tell.

"Listen to me, Bud," Fred's father interrupted. Wouldn't you feel denigrated accepting the position that I have had to leave in what was your ranch?

"Why would I feel denigrated?

"Because it would be painful for you to enter to be sent where you should be sending.

"Bah! I am a man of every moment. I did what I did convinced of its results and it doesn't weigh me down. Now I know that I cannot be more than a cowboy and I will accept it without reservation. If it's on that ranch, all the better. I have affection for him and that affection will make me work harder to defend him.

"In that case I think I can fix it, unless Lou Big, its current owner, doesn't object." As a result of my accident, he appointed Rex Milton as foreman, as he is the oldest laborer, but Rex is wide of the position. Lou is looking for a tough, authoritative foreman who knows his trade and may not disdain you.

"Well, you can speak to Mr. Big, if you see fit; but well understood that I will not accept the position if your son Fred does not enter as a pawn. I want to get this damn ass under my control, because he's a useless cowboy who can't handle a bad lasso and still needs a skirt and a nurse.

Fred stirred, yelling:

"Shut up, you fucking gunman, or I'll beat you up!

"That was what we had to talk about." Don't brag because you've beaten me many times. I just want to have you under my command now so that I have a chance to spank you as many times as you insubordinate against me.

"We'll argue with our fists, and I'm afraid Mr. Big is going to have to find a substitute foreman for when you're in bed with a swollen nose."

"Well, I accept the challenge." And now, you can move however you want to achieve that.

And old man Sanders did it. Big didn't think it a bad thing to have someone who knew the ranch by heart as a foreman, and the next day he admitted him, giving him the job in front of the whole team, of which Fred became a part.

Bud was straightforward in greeting. There were still some peons who worked under him when he was the owner and he promised to treat everyone as a partner, but demanding a return as he would have demanded if he continued to be the owner of the hacienda.

And so Bud, after that three"year odyssey, returned to the lost home, even though it was now a borrowed home.

CHAPTER II

BUD WALKS TOO FAST

For Bud it was stronger than he had supposed his entry back into the ranch. Two different and unexpected emotions collided in him, producing a feeling disorder that took a long time to digest.

The first was to recall an entire past that the dynamism of his eventful life had swept from his imagination, leaving only a slight reminiscence that at times vanished like an imprecise dream that cannot be remembered no matter how many efforts are made.

Those walls told him of his happy childhood, shaken by his grandfather Kelly, always dragging his revolver as if attached to him; of his dead mother, when he was barely seven years old, the one who had loved him as a supreme being and the one who had suffered serious doubts and deep concerns when knowing a powder ready to explode for nothing, and, ultimately, of his father , severe, but sweet and affectionate, hard in the line of duty, soft when affection overflowed and she felt herself revive in him for the future when she saw him, now almost a man, strong and tall, brave and spirited, aware of his work and promising of a life of continuation of the race.

Then ... he remembered the last night with her; when he died by a whim of fate, he lay on the white bed with his olive face dressed in an ivory patina; his limp mustaches drooping over his bloodless lips and his thin, callused hands crossed over his belly, as if he wanted to retain the last pain that had taken him from the world before enjoying the right that an era of supreme efforts at work gave him .

Perhaps this had been one of the reasons that prompted Bud to get rid of the ranch and flee the environment where so much had happened and so little connected with it could happen. Now he seemed to realize it and felt a hidden bitterness for having returned to remember something that he had buried so badly, that now it resurfaced with more bitterness and pain than when they died.

On the other hand, he found the interior of the ranch changed. Each owner has his tastes, and thus, the current one, differed a lot from the previous one, perhaps because the years change customs and tastes, as people's physiognomy changes.

However, he noticed something very subtle about this change that did not make him resentful, but rather strange. He couldn't quite define what it was; But she found it more cheerful, perhaps whiter, with refined details than she had ever seen before, and these details, of a feminine spirituality, brought her back to remembering her mother, when she was the wise and kind hand that took care of the trifle decoration of the home , in contrast to the rudeness of its inhabitants.

This detail linked him to that other new emotion that he had experienced when he returned to the ranch, and this emotion was twenty-one years old, dark, with deep black eyes, fine and swaying waist, gallantry in walking and persuasion and energy in the voice. Her name was Nancy and she was the daughter of the new owner, Lou Big.

In Bud's eventful life, women had no other significance than easily forgettable fortuitous accidents. None had crossed his path with ravishing force, and all were minor pastimes on his restless journeys through the West. If the sailors could boast that they left "a love in each port", he could parody them by affirming that in each village he had left a few hours of love affair; but the next morning the distance and the dust of the roads had erased them.

But now, when casting the definitive anchor of the ship of his existence, when faced with a single panorama that could not change or erase from his retina the impression of the things seen, the figure of Nancy, with her accused personality and her irresistible attraction. It was like a punishment for his frivolity; something that punished him to reconcentrate in an hour what he had scattered in all for a future martyrdom that God would know how he would be able to endure, and this consideration made him regret having returned and, above all, having agreed to re"enter that house, where now it was seen how it could be contemplated in an exotic mirror where the figures were projected in the opposite direction to reality.

For a moment he considered taking his horse and leaving without further ado. His character was that; but there was in him a background of a proud man who did not admit defeat without a previous fight.

If he had wanted to be the first dominator of the "Colt" in all the Colorado and he had succeeded, why should he not achieve other things as or more difficult than that?

Not to present a battle to love, as to death, would be to renounce being who he was, and rather than renounce it, he preferred to see himself in the cemetery next to his father's grave, with a bouquet of flowers on the slab and facing the sun. , or to the clouds.

On the other hand, who could be against trying? Nobody, except the one interested, and this one could also be beaten. Nancy was single, and while she was, she had lost nothing to attempt her conquest.

It is true that he had realized that that vain Laurence Raft, alleged heir of the "Caja Bonita" ranch, a property that had more of tradition in the region than of positive value, but, it was not an obstacle that bothered Bud much. . He could be eliminated in many ways, either by winning Nancy's love for good, or by disfiguring her face with fists, or by putting a couple of shots between the two eyebrows to lead him out of the idea of marrying the girl. beautiful ranchera.

And since Bud was a man born to fight and what he liked least was inactivity, he decided to stay and dedicate all his energy to two things: to earn the trust and esteem of his employer, showing him that he was the ideal man to become. charge of the hacienda in a more or less distant future, and to make Nancy fall in love, who was, ultimately, the one who should have the last word in this matter.

And since Bud was all will when he proposed it, his capturing work began the same day that he studied his situation in depth, proposing to carry out the days in double gear.

Soon old Big could see that the acquisition he had made admitting Bud as a foreman had not been a myth. The young man not only did wonders in the pastures and rodeos with the cattle, but also offered in his free hours to help him carry the books, give him advice on the markets he knew very well and on the sale of the hatajos, and this His work had a reward: Big put his complete trust in him and not only improved his salary, but also gave him the status of a man in the privacy of his home rather than a salaried employee of the same.

When circumstances permitted, Bud devoted his attentions to Nancy; sometimes it was by bringing her real mountains of country flowers, which she liked very much; others helping her to fix the infinite pots that she had installed on the railing of the upper gallery; some, teaching her riding tricks that the girl did not know, and all this always accompanied by their most exquisite smiles, very respectful phrases and elegant and restrained gestures.

This recruitment work had caused him to distance himself somewhat from the company of his inseparable Fred. Many Saturdays she gave up going down to the village to have fun like the team did, claiming different pretexts, and sometimes it was because she had promised Miss Nancy to accompany her to steal honey from the combs; others, because they were going to test the speed of a new jackfruit and others ... without giving specific explanations. One day, Fred, bored, rebuked him:

"Hey, you little yearling, how do you feel about my physique?"

"Phs! Not too bad. I know them somewhat uglier.

"Do you think that if I painted my complexion and put on some nice skirts, I would get you to pay me a little more attention?

"What the hell is that question coming to?

"Because you no longer have time or eyes except for Miss Nancy and the rest does not count for you in the world."

Bud tried to control his blush at his friend's discovery and yelled:

"Don't be silly, Fred! You mistake gallantry for the horns of the yearlings.

"And one with six years to turn you away from me! Fred added maliciously. You have your brain swallowed up by that bud and you are going to get the number one disappointment of your life. You are too high for your size.

"Because? Bud roared, beside himself.

"Because neither father nor daughter will ever want you for her husband." There are more handsome and with more money.

Bud, impetuous, advanced towards his friend and shaking him, shouted:

"Repeat that and I'll punch you in the face!

"Well, it's repeated, and now try to see if you can carry out your threat.

Bud lunged at Fred, sending him a direct shot that would undo his jaw if he caught him fully, and Fred snapped back, applying one to his chest that sent him back roaring like a tiger.

For a long time he furiously debated wanting to pound his friend's face uselessly, receiving, in return, several caresses from him that he fit in with anger, until he realized that if he persisted he was going to disfigure his face, which would make him smile. to Nancy, he gave up saying:

"It's okay. I'm not in shape today. Another day will be.

"No, if you're in shape, what happens to you is that you don't want her to point at your face and she laugh when she knows the beating I've given you." Yes, I will know you well!

Bud, gritting his teeth, confessed:

"It's okay. You're right. But one day I'll get paid. Besides, you are the one who has the least right to make fun of me.

"Who's making fun of you, you piece of ass? What I do is warn you of what can happen to you.

""Because? Am I not as much of a man as anyone else?

"But a man only has a poor rate." Instead, take, for example, Laurence Raft; It has more value.

"What do you propose? Bud roared. What look for him and put two bullets in his mouth to sour that stupid smile he has?

"God save you from doing it." Then she would resent you and the path taken would be useless.

Bud was plagued by his friend's pessimistic remarks. She had never given ground to any man in any aspect of life and she was not going to give ground to Laurence now, precisely on the most vital problem that had presented itself to her heart.

Bud pondered the situation and believed he had gained his way in the young woman's love. Nancy was happy with him and sought his company with a certain interest, which did not go unnoticed.

On more than one occasion he had postponed the proud rancher for doing some whim in conjunction with Bud, whom he recognized as more virile, more aggressive, finer in his dealings, and these details not only flattered Bud, but also gave him illusions for the future.

But aside from these warm moments of sentimentality and serenity, the young man was still the impetuous and terrible man he had always been.

In the team there were elements that had entered the Grand Canyon after their march and one of them, a Californian tall and strong as oak, who boasted of being a tough and quarrelsome man and who had already caused countless fights in the town.

Scott, who was called the peon, was distinguished more by his provocative nature than by his love of work, and Bud, who did not admit rudeness where he was, took him by the handkerchief that he wore around his neck, on the occasion of surprising him wandering through the pastures, and said, without getting upset:

"Scott, I've told you several times that you only come here to work." To contemplate the landscape, you go to the Grand Canyon, which has them beautiful, and you do not steal people's money with impunity.

Scott found the reprimand too strong, especially in front of his teammates, and, emboldening himself, replied:

"Hey, Bud, I think you're showing off a lot and I'm not a man to put up with threats from anyone."

Bud didn't deign to answer; He took him by the waist with his right hand, without letting go of the left handkerchief, raised him in the air and with a marvelous volley launched him into space to end the unexpected air trip headfirst into one of the ponds where he watered the cattle.

A chorus of loud laughter welcomed the feat, and when the humiliated peon, dripping and full of silt, managed to get out onto the mainland, he approached him saying:

"And now I'm going to make him drier than esparto in the sun, with my fists.

He knew how to apply the lessons he had received from Fred wonderfully to the face and body of the laborer, whom he left ten minutes later in the arms of his companions, so that they could try the difficult task of making him understand that he was still in the world of the living.

The feat was witnessed by Big, his daughter and Laurence Raft, who that morning had gone out with the father and daughter to the village. Big, a lover of discipline and fond of his rude foreman, did not reveal the impression that the event had produced on him; Nancy was quite moved by the aggressiveness and gallantry of the impetuous foreman, and Laurence, who boasted of being a tough man and who liked to boast of it, looked from the top of the horse to Bud, who was terribly annoyed when he discovered him near the young woman. , and commented contemptuously:

"If you had been the foreman of my ranch, you would not have allowed my peons to be treated like that." The pastures are not a gambling den where fights are justified.

Bud stirred angrily, yelling:

"Hey, Laurence, why don't you get into the things that concern you and leave the things you don't care about?" If you are fond of fighting in the gambling dens, I am not; but I am to do it where I find a man who annoys me, and you have been annoying me for a long time.

Laurence, seeing himself thus challenged in front of the girl, felt that he should show off in her presence by punishing that inferior being, whom he also hated because he was so obsequious to Nancy, and with an impetuous leap he detached himself from the horse, trying to fall on Bud. to surprise you in the fall; but that one, who was waiting for the attack, stretched out his arms, caught him in the fall, and before he could turn he had sent him to the pool, as he had sent Scott.

The posture she must have assumed when she fell was undoubtedly so extravagant that Nancy, despite the drama of the situation, could not contain a loud laugh that vibrated like a silver bell.

Bud was intimately flattered to hear her laugh, and as he approached the pond, he waited for Raft to escape from the mud and when he did, he faced him saying:

"And now I am ready to give you all the explanations you want and in the field of your choice."

Big, scared, intervened to say:

"Stop it, Bud! You have exceeded your actions. Mr. Raft is our guest and I cannot tolerate such treatment.

"Nor can I tolerate anyone outside the ranch censoring my methods of keeping the pretty children who are paid, do not work and threaten me." I don't think you pay me for that.

"Of course not. Anyway, I beg all of you to put this unpleasant incident for granted. Come on, Raft, please. Upstairs at the ranch, you can change your clothes.

Raft, through clenched teeth, muttered:

"We'll settle this one day, Bud." I am not a man who leaves bills unpaid.

"I'll pay it to you in revenue when I collect it," Bud said simply.

The situation created by these incidents scared Big a bit. Her foreman was an ideal man, but his character threatened to create serious conflict for her, especially by mediating what now mediated between him and Raft. Days later, when Saturday arrived, Bud did not want to leave the ranch, and on Sunday, alone and bored in the shed, he drew his old Mexican guitar that he had not drawn for a long time, and sitting on a bench in the patio, he dedicated himself to press it, singing old Spanish air songs, which he had learned in his rambles across the West.

Bud had an excellent baritone voice and a lot of taste and feeling when singing, and so, dominated that day by a melancholy that he could not understand where it came from, he dedicated himself to improvising songs about old Hispanic musical themes, which were always aimed at singing a song. silent and impossible love.

Once she raised her eyes to the railing where Nancy used to lean over to watch the sunsets, and with narrowed eyes, she sang:

 I have burning thistles

inside my heart;

your eyes have caught them

viciously and without compassion.

And although in the end, in my chest

only remains,

I beg you to hug me

with the glare of your eyes.

 Rancherita! ... Rancherita!

 Look at me out of compassion

until there is nothing left

of my poor heart! ...

The last stanza died in his throat in an excited tremolo, and when he least expected it, Nancy's fresh and harmonious voice, a little too excited, exclaimed from the railing:

"Very nice couplet, Mr. Raines! I did not know you so sentimental and with such a beautiful voice!

Bud, like a schoolboy caught in the dark, blushed to the whites of his eyes when he was surprised in that intimate act of his hidden feelings, and stammered:

"Oh, excuse me, I didn't know you were there!"

"And that has to do? I really liked his songs. You play the guitar very well and sing better.

"Thank you very much, Miss Nancy." I grow it little. Sometimes when I'm a little sad, I get around ...

She separated herself from the railing and went down to the patio bathed by a reflection of the moon that painted the lush vine that hugged the porch silver.

Nancy was marvelously beautiful, in a flowered robe, her hair down, and the white and turned neckline highlighted by the blue of the fabric. Bud almost fainted as he watched her move toward him in that guise and sentimental moment in his life.

Nancy walked over to him and reaching out with her ebony arm took the guitar, which Bud handed her with tremors of anguish. The girl rested her left foot on the stone bench, exposing her pretty leg, settled the guitar in her lap and after checking the temper of the strings, she strummed a Mexican song with great grace and style.

Finally, in a low voice, but with a timbre that was a compliment and encouragement, he sang:

 Manito, do not despair,

that love is a star;

the one who wants to reach her

it will go up it.

 Then, he offered the guitar to Bud, saying:

"Someday I'll have to ask you to sing for me."

He, stimulated by the couplet, believing that it was like a hidden promise, approached her asking in a low voice:

"Do you believe in the sense of that couplet?

She stared at him in the silvery gloom that enveloped him, and her eyes blazed like two coals lit in gold.

"Why not? He replied. All verses have a meaning in life.

"Yes, like all things they tend to have a difficult barrier to jump over. Who can reach a star?

"Whoever has the will, determination and spirit for it." You can get to heaven with your thought and your soul. There are things that are not tangible for the hand, but for the spirit.

"And meat doesn't count? We are human and we debate on earth. Everything that does not come from it and can satisfy us bodily does not calm our concerns.

"Then you have to stop wishing for the stars to yearn for something more mundane in life."

"Because? Is it prosaic to long for a woman's love?

"His love, no." Your love can be like a pure and shining star; but there are those who are blind and stop seeing the star to see only the envelope.

"That is left to rude spirits." I am a rough and violent man to some extent. I have had to fight against the materialism of life, because life here imposes rudeness and violence; but, precisely by contrast, I have always longed for the spirituality of something that serves as a haven to the hardened soul and that haven can only be found in a woman.

"How many have you found who have offered it to you and have scorned it?

"None. Many women marched on my path. All had allowed the mire to take over the pure waters of their soul. Mine couldn't bathe in a pond when she tried to get out of her own.

"Then console yourself." Someday you will find it.

"What if I have found it and there is a wall in front of it that prevents me from reaching it?

Nancy looked at him strangely for a moment and replied:

"Are you not a brave and risky man, for whom there are no obstacles? Well, skip it.

Bud felt inside him as if a knife had been stabbed into him, spurring his hot, fiery blood. He looked for a moment at Nancy, who stood in front of him beautiful, seductive, provocative, and, unable to contain the momentum that was driving him forward, he threw himself on her, grabbed her by the waist and in a feverish movement sought her mouth to stamp. in her a kiss that was like the total surrender of her soul consuming herself with love. Nancy began an instinctive backward movement, as if trying to evade the outrage; but he could not and his red and warm lips felt the devouring fire of that kiss.

Suddenly, a harsh and harsh voice broke the charm of the sublime moment, stating angrily:

"You scoundrel! ... You will tell me of the outrage you have committed with Miss Big!

Bud abruptly released the young woman, who drew back at the threatening voice, and found herself face to face with Laurence, who, with his hand on the butt of the revolver, stabbed at him with his eyes, in which he blazed. the flame of the most concentrated hatred.

Bud stiffened. He had taken off his belt and carried no weapon.

Tensing his muscles, he replied:

"How do you want me to respond to your challenge if you have weapons and I don't?

"Of course, to insult a woman they weren't accurate; to fight a man it is better not to wear them and thus fear is better hidden.

Bud was shaking with anger when he heard those phrases. No man had ever allowed himself to launch such an insult and much more in front of a woman like the one who for him was everything in life.

Advancing intrepidly, he replied:

"Shoot! Shoot now, and kill me cowardly if that's what you mean, or let me fight with your own weapons! I have the revolver in the shed.

Laurence, who was not a coward even if he was a fool, unbuckled his belt, tossed it into a corner, and said:

"I am not a murderer." I am nobler than you, for I do not outrage a woman and fight men face to face. You treacherously threw me into the pond the other day. Let's see if now, without advantages, he is able to beat me like then.

Bud saw heaven open with that offering. He hated Laurence, but had no choice but to admire his honesty and set out to fight him nobly.

"Thank you," he said. Otherwise I would have killed him. From this I will settle for applying a severe punishment. They both stood guard and studied each other, ready to fight roughly and to the last limit. They were staring at the woman who was everything in their lives, and while they did not know who would be decided by, they were willing to do whatever they could to tip the balance in their favor.

Laurence was taller and heavier than Bud, but Bud possessed tremendous agility, highly cultivated toughness, and a rage that surpassed that of his enemy.

It was Laurence, the most angry and nervous, who initiated the attack, and Bud soon realized that he was not a despicable enemy. He knew many boxing rules and it was not an easy task to surprise him.

But he had also learned many things from Fred, who at the cost of forcing him to take very hard blows, had taught him tricks and rules that he could not forget, and thus, dodging the harsh onslaught of his rival, he quickly turned around him to tire him and to break down the hardness of his blows with fatigue.

Laurence was the first to make the hardness of his fist felt. Glancingly he brushed against Bud's forehead, who thought he had been hit by a piece of rock, but was able to dodge the full swing and escape with that half"caress.

Soon he could see that, from a distance, Laurence was a terrible opponent, whose guard was difficult to break. Always with his arms at face level, he covered his chin and from time to time he stretched, like a spring, his right arm, looking for the face of his enemy, who had to avoid blows with a hard game of waist or with feline jumps, without being able to touch his adversary.

This enraged him. He remembered Fred's tactic and remembered that he could only break him with short combat and getting into his enemy's turf.

Exposing himself to a rough blow, he jumped up and into Laurence's guard, hitting him in the liver.

The rancher, although he wanted to flee, did not succeed, for Bud stuck to him like a limpet to stone, and then he was forced to accept the combat on the ground that was offered, looking for a way to annul his adversary.

But he had dealt hard blows to the liver and heart that broke Laurence's strength, and now the fight was even, for the rancher, accusing the blows, was panting like a bull after a long run.

When they parted, Bud had a black eye from a short hook thrown at him, but Laurence doubled over in pain and covered himself with difficulty.

Hot and blinded by the blows they received, they threw themselves fully in a supreme desire to eliminate themselves quickly, and now they were only careful to try to deliver final blows rather than to cover themselves from receiving them.

Bud was bleeding from one ear and had a black eye; Laurence had a split eyebrow and puffy lips, but neither gave up and the two of them were doubling their efforts looking for the end of the fight.

Laurence, feeling faint, sought the coup de grace to the chin of his enemy and stretched out his arm in a withering way seeking his face; But Bud was able to dodge in time and the rancher's arm floated over his shoulder, forcing him to lean forward, leaning almost on Bud's chest. He rejected him with his left hand, and with his right he crushed his face, throwing him backwards as if driven by a gale.

Like a lifeless mass, it fell backwards, crashing headlong into the hard stones of the patio, and there it lay, showing no signs of life.

Panting, Bud straightened up and, after running his hand over his face to wipe away the blood that was blinding him, tried to smile and turned his eyes to the porch where Nancy had retreated, speechless with excitement from the terrible fight she had just fought. witness; but when he was about to start a friendly smile towards her, the smile was frozen on his lips.

Standing on the porch steps, arms folded and cold and commanding, was Big, who, slowly descending the ladder, approached Bud, saying icily:

"This is intolerable, Mr. Raines." I warned you the other day that I was not prepared to allow my guests to be treated in this way in my own house, and you have dared to repeat the action again. What do you have to argue in your favor?

Bud shot an anguished look at Nancy, who stood leaning against the wall like a statue of ice, and lowering her eyes submissively replied:

"Nothing, Mr. Big." You are right and my duty is to abide by your decisions. The reasons he could cite are so personal that he would reveal them to no one in the world.

He turned to go and when he discovered the guitar leaning against the wall, he took it; He stared at it for a moment, then slammed it against the bench, disappearing into the shed.

CHAPTER III

BIG PREPARES A TRAP

Mr. Big, amazed, looked at his daughter, who, shrugging her shoulders and without saying a word, disappeared across the porch, and Big, stunned, guessing something strange in that attitude and in that duel, called the cook, who came hurried.

"John. He said, "Help me take this man to the basin to cool him down." Then find me the medicine cabinet. Between them they submerged him in the cold water for more than half an hour, until at last Laurence seemed to begin to show signs of life.

Big, then, gave orders to transfer him to one of the ranch rooms, and taking the first"aid kit that John presented him, he washed the wounds, applied iodine compresses and bandaged him as best he could, until he was a little presentable.

When he did not know what else to do for him, he left him in a heavy drowsiness and moved to his office, where he made his daughter come.

This, guessing that one of the most decisive moments of her life had come for her, came with clenched teeth and distracted eyes. His thought was much further away than his body from that narrow enclosure.

Big, who adored his daughter and who for her would have been capable of the greatest sacrifices, indicated a chair in front of him and then asked:

"Let's see, Nancy, you who witnessed the fight, tell me what you obeyed."

After a moment's hesitation, she replied in a firm voice:

"Dad: a man has told you that his reasons were so personal that he would reveal them to no one in the world. Why should I be the one to betray those feelings?

"I don't care about that boastful kind." People do not fight for the pleasure of fighting in front of a woman, especially when that woman has a very close friendship with one of the contestants.

"Of course not; but those are his things. If Laurence thinks otherwise, let him be the one to tell you.

"You are declining? Don't you trust me enough to tell me?

"Yes; but it is a matter of two men. Let them speak if they deem it pertinent. I, for my part, approve of the attitude of your foreman.

He approached the girl and, putting his hand on her shoulder, asked affectionately:

"Was it because of you?

"Would you dislike it?

"I dont know. I think so, because neither of them just filled me up.

"Don't you say Bud is a magnificent man?"

"As a foreman, yes." Like something else, no. He does not have a dollar, he is such an impulsive and quarrelsome man that he would be capable of treating you like cattle or like men who are not nice to him; and as for Laurence, he is not a bad game, he has a good type, he is relatively rich, but he is a fool and I don't think he has much to hide in his head.

"I wonder if the same thing happens in his heart," she replied, with a vagueness whose meaning Big could not decipher.

"Are you persistent in hiding what happened from me?

"I've already told you it's theirs." If Laurence thinks he should reveal it to you, let him do so.

"Well. That does not mean that I suspect that you have been the cause of the fight.

"Suspect what you want, Dad;" But as long as you don't know for sure, don't ring the bells flying.

And, turning around, he left the office, leaving his father plunged into a sea of confusion.

The next morning, when Laurence was in a position to realize reality, the rancher came to the ranch to inquire about his condition, and Laurence, cursing like a cowboy, exclaimed:

"Thank you very much for your interest, sir, but I suspect that you have not thought very well, of me letting myself be spanked again by that damned foreman, the devil confuse it." He has fists of steel and he brought me down carelessly. Anyway, I console myself because I know that I also gave him his.

"It was so, dear, but ... do you want to tell me what the fight was about?"

Laurence stared at him in amazement for a moment, then replied:

"Have you asked him?

"Yes, but you refused to tell me."

Laurence, impetuous, without measuring his words, said:

"Of course he would refuse! What he did was not done by honest men and that is why he kept it for himself; but I have no problem telling him. I caught him kissing Miss Nancy and felt compelled to come to her defense.

Big stiffened at the rancher's statement. If so, why hadn't Nancy been as indignant as he was, and why had she not revealed it to him by indignantly demanding that he immediately be thrown off the ranch?

Big guessed a lot of things in a moment. He understood the dignified attitude of Bud assuming responsibility for the fight without discovering the causes, so as not to question Nancy; He guessed that she had not been very offended by the loving treatment she had received from him and felt a certain revulsion towards Laurence knowing that he was so vain that he did not admit the possibility that another man could have more influence over his daughter than he and, in a contemptuous tone, I ask:

"Did you stop to inquire whether my daughter liked your involvement in her personal affairs?

Laurence, as if spoken in an incomprehensible language, looked wide"eyed at the rancher and exclaimed:

"But Mr. Big ... can you assume your daughter ...?"

"I don't suppose anything." I will limit myself to asking you whether you obtained authorization from her to defend your jurisdiction.

"Of course not! I honestly assumed that ...

"I think you made a regrettable mistake, Mr. Raft, and that you have aggravated the matter by revealing the origin of the fight." Neither Bud wanted to tell me, nor did my daughter. If that doesn't tell you anything ...

Laurence, disconsolate, rose laboriously from his bed and exclaimed:

"Oh, God! ... Is it possible that ...?

"Nothing is possible and everything is possible." I think you are very broken from that beating that could have been avoided by not getting involved in a matter for which no one had given you authorization and I think the best thing is that you dedicate yourself to taking care of yourself calmly. I'm going to order that the gig be hooked up to transfer him to his ranch, and I hope the thing is nothing serious.

Laurence was about to reply, but the emotion was such that he fell back on the pillow, breathing heavily.

Big left the room and, going to his office, called his daughter. This, intrigued, responded to the call. Big, appearing calm, said:

"I've just come to see Laurence." He's better now and can be transferred to his ranch.

"I'm glad. I think that bad time could be avoided.

"I have told you that, too," the rancher stated simply.

Nancy looked at him intensely for a moment, and then she lowered her eyes, a little flushed, not daring to say a word.

Big, excited, approached her and asked:

"What do you have to tell me now?

"Nothing but one thing." That he has so little to hide in his head as in his heart.

"We agree; but that does not prevent the situation from being somewhat equivocal. Now there is nothing to hide, Nancy, and that is why you have the floor.

"Thanks Dad; but I really don't know what to tell you ...

"I don't think it's much." He kissed you ...

"I do not deny it...

"What did you do to stop it?

"Nothing. I did not have time.

"later?

"I didn't have time to think about it." Laurence intervened so suddenly that I couldn't think.

"Good, but now ...

"I think it's too late." Don't you think?

"I think the one who doesn't like it is you." Do you really love him?

"You ask me a difficult question, Dad." He is a man I have always liked. He has behaved in a noble and courteous way, he has treated me with elegance and distinction, he has endeavored to make my life pleasant in many moments and I have had nothing to reproach him for.

"Let go of the matter, my daughter." The moment...

"Well, the moment is very confusing." There is something in his favor: he has been more gentleman and more discreet than Laurence. He will allow himself to be fired from the ranch without alleging anything in his favor. Not even that I was the involuntary cause of his excess. He sang his melancholy to the beat of the guitar and

I went like the quail to the claim. We chat. He hinted at an impossible love, perhaps I would give him a foothold for his action. The damage is already done.

“Not yet. Two solutions remain. Either you like him, and the thing is formalized, or I must fire him immediately.

“Is the reason so serious that you deprive yourself of such a useful element?

“The reason, no, since you don't complain; what may happen next, yes.

“What can happen?

"Let him repeat the action." I would do it instead. A kiss has only two solutions: either a slap or another kiss. Apart from that, I have a feeling that the matter with Laurence is not going to remain like this. Raft is tough and, if he knows he is defeated, he will try to claim the affront. Today it was with fists, but tomorrow it could be with shots, and if it is with shots ... I will prepare the crown of myrtles that adorns Raft's grave.

Nancy paled at her father's statement and, all agitated, asked:

“What solution do you find, dad?

“Several; but it all depends on what you decide.

“If I can't decide! I was surprised by this. I don't know if Bud really has a crush on me!

“What do you need to know, to take you by the hair and drag you to see the shepherd?

"Not so much, Dad." On the other hand, I need to study the case. I like it, I confess it; but ... you say that he is poor, that he is violent, you fear that his treatment of me is ... that of a vulgar cowboy. There are many drawbacks, on your part.

"To hell with what I might think, dear!" It is you who decides your happiness. Think about it and your resolution depends on two solutions that I have.

"Tell me."

“If you don't like him, fire him, and if you like him ...

“The fact that?

“Listen to me. I just received bad news that, deep down, is good for you. Your Uncle Ben is dead.

“   Poor Uncle Ben! Nancy exclaimed, genuinely pained. He was very good to me, but he had a terrible temper.

"Yes, he died of a tantrum, the sheriff of Whitebilis tells me." He has not been able to digest the fact that the cattle rustlers "dented" a good tip of cattle, and between that, the rheumatism that did not allow him to move with the relief he was used to and the hard and unmanageable equipment that he has on the ranch, they have contributed to his death. Your uncle has believed to be doing you a favor by leaving you heir to that cattle"raising hell and appoints you as the universal heir to his assets; But just as the ranch is good and could be profited from, it is a hornet's nest that neither you nor any woman nor many men can govern. It takes an exceptional guy who sleeps with the "Colt" in his hand and puts the team around his waist and kills the cattle rustlers that take refuge in the Wilson Mountains, very affordable to provide shelter, and that ...

"And that guy is ...

"Bud Raines."

"What do you mean by that?

"That if you really like him, we can put him to the test." You don't have a dollar; But if he cleanses the ranch of undesirables and makes it prosper, he will have earned a woman like you and the right to enjoy prosperity that will be due to his efforts alone. This is my other solution. Think about it and decide.

Nancy got up, ready to go.

"Let me study it, Dad." This is very serious.

"A lot, but don't be late." I have to make a decision with that wild colt and everything that will later embolden him.

Nancy, when she got to the door, turned and said smiling:

"Okay, but while I'm studying it ... I think you should propose it to him, see if he accepts."

And he fled like a doe, while his father smiled in a strange way.

Bud spent one of the most terrible nights of his life, pondering his situation.

He was not afraid of being fired from the ranch, he presumed that this was the only viable measure that Big could take with him after the offense he had inflicted on his daughter; but it did cause him the most intense anguish to think that he had gone too far in his impulses and that now he had lost all possibilities of nobly conquering her love.

Sometimes, tormented by shame, he felt the impulse to get up, take his horse and flee, but a mysterious force nailed him to the mat, preventing him from doing so. Sunday was no more pleasant for him. He was surprised that he had not yet received notice from the rancher to appear before him and make his liquidation, but, considering the case, it was said that perhaps he did not know the causes of the fight and if Nancy, out of blush, had hidden them, he would not judge so serious his fight with Laurence and was calmly thinking about the attitude he should take with him.

The downside was if the spiteful rancher spoke up and gave Big a background on the reason for the fight. If this happened and it was only known, through his mouth, causing the girl the discredit that was to be supposed, he promised to shoot the charlatan where he found him,

When Sunday night arrived and late, the team returned and with him Fred, who had gone down to town to have fun for a while.

Fred, very cheerful, went into the shed where Bud slept in isolation and, leaning on the doorjamb,

"What's up, old fox? How are you doing with your bouts of melancholy?

Bud snorted at him, and leaping forward with clenched fists, roared:

"Get out of my sight, Fred! Take off, if you don't want me to blow up those vulture snouts.

"That would have to see! Fred replied cheerfully. You are not capable of placing a fist in the trunk of an elephant.

An enraged Bud lunged at him with a direct shot, but Fred dodged sharply and his fist slammed into the doorjamb.

The furious foreman roared like a wounded bull, but as he turned and stood in the lantern light that dimly illuminated the shed, Fred saw the marks of the fighting on his face.

"By the horns of a cow, Bud! Who the hell drew that map on your face?

"Who won't be in a position to brag about it for a long time! Bud snapped grumpily.

The pawn approached Bud and, dropping his wide hand on the young man's shoulder, exclaimed:

"I'm sorry, Bud, I didn't know you had a fight." Who was the lucky mortal? Do not tell me. I already know it.

"Because?

"Because it could only have been Laurence."

"What do you base yourself on for it?

"In that he is the only one who casts a shadow on your heart."

Bud grabbed the headboard and threw it at his head, but Fred caught it in midair and handed it back, hitting him on the head.

"Don't be a slutty mule, Bud;" nor for this you are good. Do you want to stop playing the ass and tell me what happened?

"Nothing that might interest anyone but me." I'll just tell you one thing: I'm leaving this ranch tomorrow.

Fred whistled in a peculiar way and asked:

"Are you leaving or are they kicking you out?

"For the case, it's the same." I'm leaving and that's it.

"Have you thought about where?

"To the hell! The young man yelled desperately.

"Well, that's what you could continue here for." Well, after all, in hell I hope we won't be too bad.

Bud turned irate.

"What are you saying? He roared.

"That we won't be so bad there." I'm tired of beans, collard greens, smoked bacon, and all the other ingredients. Hope hell dishes have more sauce.

Bud, excited by Fred's attitude, approached him saying:

"Not. You will not go. Nothing goes against you. You have your father here and you must ...

"Fuck your advice, Bud!" Do you think I can leave you alone for the world? What for, so that the first one that comes your way will knock you off? No, sonny, you are condemned to carry a babysitter behind you and that babysitter has to be me.

Bud, tired of Fred's ironies, said:

"Don't be persistent, Fred, I won't admit it." My affairs do not have to disturb anyone's life. I'll go alone and if they spank me, console yourself; You have done it so many times that one more does not matter.

"Of course it matters, sonny." That I beat you is fine, but that others steal that glory from me, no. Get this over your head.

Bud roared, kicked, threatened, but to no avail. Fred stood his ground and when he got tired of hearing him, he went to the door and yelled from it:

"Goodbye, calf! Muge all you want, you will get tired. I hope that when morning comes tomorrow, you have remained speechless and it is easier to argue with you.

And slamming the door, he disappeared.

Around eight in the morning, when Bud had been up for two hours and with his duffel ready for the march, Fred showed up at the shed. She had dressed for a holiday and carried the bundle of her clothes under her arm.

"Anytime, old fox," he said. The soles of my feet prick from stepping on weeds on this damn ranch.

Bud was about to retort violently, when the pawn who served as the cook showed up at the shed, saying:

"Bud, the boss calls you into his office."

Bud hesitated for a moment, but, coming to a resolution, he warned Fred:

"Wait a bit, I'll come down soon." I think it is better to face the situation.

Fred winked expressively and warned:

"And no fists, sweetie."

CHAPTER IV

BUD ACCEPTS A PROPOSAL

Steadily, Bud entered the rancher's office. This one, behind his desk, had a large pile of papers spread out on the board, and although he remained with his head bowed, he was examining Bud's face through, studying his reactions.

Finally, she raised her head and looking at him severely exclaimed:

"Mr. Raines, on Saturday you were unaware of the reasons for your quarrel with Mr. Raft, but last night, get over them and ..."

"Sorry, Mr. Big." I think I can spare you all the explanations, especially when it comes to my dismissal. I had anticipated his idea and was only waiting to be able to communicate it to him and to place myself at his orders if he had to demand something of me in the private field.

"I hope that doesn't mean he's willing to give him a chance to shoot me to death." I am no longer the one who was once handling a gun.

Bud blushed and was quick to say:

"I think you judge me very poorly, although you have certain reasons for it." I never dreamed of that and I am only willing to let myself be shot against a wall if you think it can satisfy your self"esteem.

"And what the hell would I get by shooting you like a baby boy? Is it all you can think of to save critical situations?

"I confess that I do." Maybe this is because of my violent nature.

"But fortunately, we all don't have a powder keg in our veins like you." Please sit down and listen to me well. Do you want to tell me why you did that?

""""The fact that? Dust off Laurence?

"Not. I already know that. I mean ... the other ...

Bud blushed, replying curtly:

"Will I have to be violent to tell him?

"You'll just have to tell me." Or is it that you think I have raised my daughter to be a distraction to the first one that strikes her?

Bud, impetuous, jumped from the seat saying:

"I don't allow her to say that, not for her or for me." It is true that I could not contain myself and I kissed her. I didn't stop to think if she would like it or not, but I can tell her that I did it dominated by a deep passion that I feel towards her.

"On what grounds?

"I ignore it. It was a matter of environment. The night was so poetic ... she was so beautiful and I was so melancholic ... I had sung, without realizing it, for her. She heard him and went down to the patio, talking to us about loves, loves as impossible as reaching for the stars. She also sang a couplet to the sound of my guitar; it was a song full of encouragement and hope. I thought ... well; I foolishly believed that I could dare and I dared. I don't want to blame her, understand me well, but it gave me a footing for the case. You already know everything.

Big listened to him somewhat moved by the accent of passion and sincerity that the boy put into his story and when he finished he said, in an uncertain voice:

"Have you stopped to reflect on whether you can be worthy of your love?

The question took Bud so by surprise that it took him a long time to answer. Finally he stated:

"I do not know. I honestly think not. I am poorer than a rat.

"Let's put the money aside." There are things that have no market value and one is love. I mean your personal clothes.

"Well, in that field, I don't think there is anything to oppose me."

"Not? And that quarrelsome and dominating character that you possess? And those brusque and authoritarian manners? And that history of a man who was born with the "Colt" in his hand and who must go down to the grave with it between his fingers? Is that a virtue?

"Maybe it isn't, but in this region where the Colt is the foundation of life ...

"It will be to fight with men, but not to walk around the home with a sensitive and delicate woman. I'm afraid you are not the right man for my daughter under those conditions.

"I have not had a proper home and no one can predict how I should behave in it."

"You are going to tell me that there it will be the man who lets himself be beaten by his wife, isn't that right?"

"Not so much, but I can be the loving, tender and blissful man that she can dream of."

"I'd like to see it."

"Take the test yourself! Bud dared to say unconsciously.

"There are tests that later have no solution if they fail. Have you pondered it? You could do it, but the preliminary conditions were going to seem too harsh to you.

Bud when he heard that, the most unexpected thing he could hear, he got up again impetuously and shouted:

"What do you say?

"I seem to have spoken clearly, Mr. Raines."

This one, red as a poppy, replied:

"Well. Submit me to the test of air and fire and I will know how to respond to them in spades. I can't say more.

Big smiled and forcing him to sit up, said:

"Listen to me well, Bud." You are a boy with very good qualities, but you have some obnoxious qualities that if you don't correct them they won't get you far. I cannot promise you anything immediate, but I can promise you something for the future that it is up to you to shorten.

"My daughter has not been very indignant with you for what has been done, but neither has she started jumping for joy. She is nice, she keeps kind memories of you that make her look at you with pleasure, but she fears, like me, that This is a mask or an outburst without consistency. On the other hand, you are poor and you are, because you wanted to be. Today life demands a certain equality that you do not have, but that you can have if you want. things: to raise a share of fortune that equals her, and to finish winning her love, if it is true that you feel in love with my daughter.

"What do you do since you don't tell me those conditions? Cried Bud desperately.

"Calm down and don't let your inner beast show up, because that's the first one you have to tame." I will explain them to you, but I have already warned you that they will be harsh. My daughter, in case she lacked something to distance herself from you even more financially, has just inherited a ranch. It was left to him by his uncle Ben, his mother's brother, but that ranch is something like if he had inherited a cobra and had to feed it on his breasts. If there is something demonic in this world, it is Ben Hays' ranch, located in Whitebills, near the Wilson Mountains ..., do you know Gambling?

"Something. It is not a highly recommended part of the region.

"No, it is not. If you add to that that Ben's equipment is rougher than a wild horse, that there are cattlemen who "dent" cattle with almost impunity and that this needs to be straightened out and cleaned up, you will understand that inheritance is a gift from God.

"Well then, there is the bone to crack We can honestly value the ranch at what it is currently worth, and if within a year you commit to restore it, have a decent team, put an end to the cattle rustlers and double the value of The cattle, all that surplus, apart from the salary assigned to you, will go to your benefit to bring you to the level of my daughter and to be able to aspire to her hand. This is the material part; the spiritual part is in your charge, well understood that In order to earn your love, I do not have to give you advice, but rather take it yourself.

Bud, who was listening to the words of the rancher like one who listens to pleasant music in his ear, got up calmly asking:

"When can I leave for the ranch?

"I think as soon as you are ready." I have prepared all the papers for you to take possession of it on behalf of my daughter and a power of attorney of yours, so that no one doubts your authority. The rest is your responsibility.

Bud stepped forward, asking:

"Is it in my powers to be able to take Fred Sanders with me?

"Well. If it gets in your way and wishes you an early death, take it away; but warn yourself before.

"Needless. Fred is looking forward to finding someone who can break the lump out of his nose and I am more looking forward to this than he is. If you are not extorted, this afternoon we are going there.

"None. From this moment you are free to do so.

Bud was puzzled for a moment and then asked:

"Do you give me permission to give these same assurances to your daughter and say goodbye to her?

Big hesitated for a moment and finally said:

"I would not do it. It could be a disappointing farewell. Leave her with the memory of the other night and let her savor it, to see if she digests it well. Perhaps in a while, when she learns of her work and the sacrifices you are making for her and her interests, the interview will be more enjoyable for you.

"Well, I understand your idea and I abide by it." Say goodbye to her and assure her that I will do everything in my power to turn it into an earthly paradise, where only flowers bloom in its path and where the value of each foot of land is something that makes the most powerful pale with envy.

And shaking the rancher's hand effusively, he left the office like a madman, his eyes full of laughing landscapes of love and happiness.

When he got to the shed where Fred was waiting for him bored and melancholic, he gave him a terrible push that threw him on the mat and shouted:

"Get out of my sight, you piece of ass! ... What are you doing standing there?

"Waiting for your return ... Where have the slaps been that you don't notice?"

"Nowhere yet, but they will come." Get ready, we're leaving.

"Wow ... Have you already convinced yourself that you can't walk around the world without a babysitter?

"No: I'm going to take you to a place where I'll have to be your babysitter.

"I'd like to see it!

"Well, you will see it and, what is worse, you will feel it." We're going to a place where bullets will rain like hail and where your fists won't do the damn thing.

"I'd like to see it! Repeated stoic Fred

"Am I not telling you that you are going to see and feel it, you little yearling?

"Well, where are we going to eat the foremen like you without seasoning?"

"To Whitebills."

Fred whistled through his teeth and grumbled:

"To that accursed corner of hell, where we went out on horseback that famous Christmas night?

"Justly.; but with the particularity that now we are going to throw all those who are not welcome there.

"Is Mr. Big the one who sent you?

"Yes. I'm going to run the ranch of her brother"in"law Ben, who has died and left it to Nancy.

"To Nancy! ... But what familiarity is that, Bud? So Mr. Big lacks the courage to kill you and sends you to have others do the work on their own? Let me go upstairs and pinch his nose, for miserable!

Bud had to make heroic efforts to restrain his partner. He understood that this was a despicable task and intended to avenge her in advance.

At last he managed to convince the pawn, assuring:

"Be still, ass." What do you know the favor he's going to do me with that?

"Favor? Not that he was going to grant his daughter's hand as a prize!

Bud, unable to control the joy that overflowed in his soul, exclaimed:

"What if it were?

Fred shot him a direct shot that nearly hit him and muttered:

"Ah, indecent pig! And did you keep it quiet? And for that you looked so desperate and so closed? You deserve to have your chin broken off for a scoundrel.

"Come on, Fred, don't be spiteful." I swear it was something as great as it was unforeseen, I'll tell you about it.

The pawn scratched his head and then sheepishly asked:

"Hey, really, if you don't get jerked there, that could be your prize?"

"That's what the boss has assured me."

"You want to do me a favor?

"Tell me.

"Ask him if he extends it to me." I too am biting the halter for Rosa, Miss Nancy's maid; but she...

"Well, maybe his influence will come to that." Although it seems to me that you must be too violent for his character. If you were a calm and sensible man like me!

Fred threw a header at him, but Bud deftly dodged it.

By mid"afternoon they had everything ready for departure, and Bud went up to Big's office to say goodbye to Big.

The rancher gave him his liquidation, all the papers concerning the ranch, the authorization naming him his only representative in it and a duplicate copy of the contract that both had to sign to formalize their commitment.

"You don't have to sign it right now," Big warned. Study it and, if it suits you, sign it, and if there is a clause to discuss ...

"So that? Neither you nor I are rustlers. If we agree on the basics, on the secondary we will not disagree.

He shook old Big's hand and went down to the patio, where Fred was waiting for him on horseback.

Bud got into his and stepped off the fence. The sun was pouring down the flown gallery of the ranch and the flowers in Nancy's pots were ablaze with light and color.

The boy raised his eyes to the railing looking for the beautiful silhouette of the young woman, but he could not discover her. No doubt he held a grudge for what had happened that night.

Melancholic, he set off down the valley.

Fred wryly asked:

"Didn't you see her, Bud?

"How was he going to see her if he didn't show up? Bud replied sadly.

"No, you piece of ass. What happens is that it was leaning on the other side of the facade. I saw her looking through the glass. You're a blind man, Bud, and I'm afraid you'll never know how to win her over.

CHAPTER V

AN ENTRANCE TOO LOUD

Bud and Fred's entry into the "Cruz Alta" ranch in Whitebills was not exactly as apotheosis as the one Washington had one day in Annapolis when it returned victorious from the English. Lowell Winant, ranch foreman, came out to meet them at the fence, and when Bud asked who was in charge of the ranch, he boastfully came forward to answer:

"I am the manager, stranger, what was offered to you?"

"Just taking over the ranch on behalf of Miss Nancy Big, from whom I bring written powers."

Bud made as if to show his documentation, but the foreman, rejecting the gesture, said:

"I'm sorry you took such a troublesome walk from Grand Canyon; but here you have nothing to do. I await the visit of that young lady to understand myself with her and the rest does not satisfy me.

Bud calmly dismounted from the horse, being followed by Fred, and going over to Lowell, said:

"And do you think that Miss Nancy has such bad taste that she takes this walk to see you that "rustler" face that you have?

Lowell stiffened at the insult and fiercely replied:

"Listen, stranger." You are an operetta cowboy who comes here believing that you are going to swallow the earth, and it is easy for that to happen if it takes five minutes to disappear all the way. You need men of my size to run this ranch, and I'm not one of those who will give up the job to the first guy who comes forward to claim it.

"That means you will only give it up by force ..."

"You sound like a fortune teller."

"Oh well! In that case there is no more to talk about. Fred, would you please show this gentleman the documents that accredit you as foreman of this ranch. Fred, very amused, asked:

"Which eye do you want him to swallow: the left or the right?

"Since he's myopic, I think because of both of us."

Fred took a step forward, and Lowell, very conceited at the show he was planning to give his team, who surrounded him laughing in advance at the failure of the two strangers, arched his legs, clenched his fists, and prepared to greet Fred with dignity.

He started some odd turns with his arms, and suddenly, before Lowell had time to realize it, he was hit in the mouth, knocking out half a dozen teeth.

The foreman let out an impressive roar and leaned back, overcome with pain, while Fred, addressing Bud, excused himself by saying:

"Sorry I covered your mouth a little earlier." I am annoyed by chickens that cackle so much before they know if they are going to lay their eggs. Now I will make you "see" my credentials in due form.

Lowell, spitting blood, recovered somewhat, for he was a man of extraordinary toughness, and launched himself like a blind bull at Fred, but it did not take long to acknowledge the proper reception.

Fred's fist, like a mace, searched his right eye and with a terrible impact, he left it closed for a long season.

Despite the harsh punishment, the foreman did not give up. He knew the end that awaited him and he was making one last effort to get rid of that exceptional being, the only way to expel them from the ranch and continue to rule in it as was his project.

But Fred, who was annoyed by such obstinacy, decided to end the fight, and looking for the hard chin of the cowboy, he dealt him a final blow, which left him lying on the ground like a bundle.

Then he smiled at Bud, who had had a lot of fun admiring the strength of his friend's fists, this time at his expense, and asked:

"Is it understood that I should do the same with all this rabble, one by one, or is it enough as a small sample?

"That, they will say, Fred." You are the foreman of this ranch, by my designation, and I will not be the one to teach you how to treat your men. In any case, ask them to see what they think.

"Well, the question is asked."

The pawns looked at each other with infinite rage, until one, seeming to interpret the feelings of his companions, came forward, saying:

"We don't recognize a foreman other than Lowell."

"Which means you're leaving here immediately, doesn't it?"

"It doesn't mean more than what I said," said the menacing pawn.

Fourteen tough and determined men grinned sinisterly with their hands resting on the butts of their 'Colts', ready to support their claim, weapons in hand, but before they had time to draw them, two revolvers appeared in Bud's hands with the speed of a machine gun and ten hats of as many peons they flew through the air, torn off by the ten well"aimed bullets.

Bud, not showing the slightest tremor in his hand, warned:

"To talk to me, the first thing you have to do is discover yourself." Fred, please discover those other four.

Fred, also wielding his weapons, fired quickly. Three hats flew through the air; but the fourth had worse fortune, because he fell, his forehead pierced by a bullet.

It was the pawn who had dared refuse to follow Bud's orders.

"Sorry, Bud," Fred said, "I got out of hand."

None, faced with that test of skill and speed, dared to move a hand. Bud had already reloaded his revolvers and was waiting for the answer.

The peons, humiliated, limited themselves to heading towards the door ready to march.

"Okay," said one. There you stay with the ranch, and we will see if in a month you will retain those fumes and that ability to shoot.

Bud let them go. He had a bitter problem when he ran out of equipment to tend the cattle; but he hoped to supply him with the help of the sheriff, to whom he was well recommended.

The ranch was left with nothing but a lame old farmhand, whom the late Ben had made cook when he broke his leg in a rodeo.

Bill, who was called the peon, professed great affection for the deceased in spite of his peculiarities and his acidity of character, and had never made common cause with Lowell and his men, who did not give him great importance either.

Bud, thinking he was left alone, turned to Fred, saying:

"Try to tie me tight to this bird so it doesn't run away before I realize what it's done at the ranch since the old man's death, and then peek around the kitchen a bit to see what you can find to eat."

Fred was about to carry out the order, when a grotesquely moving bundle emerged from one of the sheds, and Bud, spotting it, stepped forward, saying:

"Who the hell are you?

"I'm the cook, sir." He was hiding there while the fireworks were going on.

"Well. What do you do that doesn't follow everyone's path?

"I have no interest in it." I was old Ben's cook and I was very fond of him. I serve the ranch, not Lowell.

"Which means he stays."

"And delighted that you wiped that leprosy off the ranch." If you took fifteen more days to come, you would not have found even the smell of cattle here.

"Very well. I will consider this act of loyalty to you, and your decent attitude will not weigh you down. See if there is anything out there that you can put in your mouth.

"Of course there is." I was preparing to prepare dinner for those lazy people, and don't think they were not living the good life.

The cook retired to his post, and Fred set about solidly binding Lowell, then locking him in one of the sheds.

"Well. He said, "That one's already saved." What the hell am I doing with this other guy now?

"He will have to be buried as God intended." Take care of that and also take care of opening an extraordinary expense account to pass it on to Mr. Big at the end of the month. There are things that must go at your expense.

"What the hell do you count as extraordinary expenses?

"Well, the value of fourteen bullets we used this afternoon and what a decent crown is worth for that guy." I like to do things methodically.

"Devil! ... It seems to me that then what the ranch yields will be spent on gunpowder.

"That's your account." I have come to run your farm, but not to spend my salary on gunpowder and bullets. Do not forget.

"Well well; it will be done as ordered by the pattern.

While the cook was preparing dinner, Bud went up to the ranch and set about examining it with Fred. The building, very abandoned and dirty, looked like a pigsty, and everything indicated that its owner, who had been held in an armchair for many months without being able to move, had been at the mercy of those rascals who had made their farm what they wanted.

"This sucks, Fred." I'm afraid you have to do a lot of work with the broom and the buckets.

"And hell with your soul, Bud." Why have you brought me here: to be a maid or a foreman?

"But don't you see how this is?

"Find a maid to take care of it." Ah ...! and see to it that he has a slightly more attractive face than that horrible foreman. I like the decoration in the rooms.

"For you to make love to her, isn't that it?"

"Me? Do not delirium. I am a decent man. For me there are no more women in the world than seven. One is Rosa and ...

"The others are already dead, Fred." I'll hire a witch and keep an eye on you just in case. I don't trust much of your scruples when it comes to skirts ...

Fred grimaced with resignation and the two of them went into the office.

Bud took out a small key that Big had given him. This corresponded to the drawer of Ben's table, where he kept his books.

Bud sent Fred to find out if dinner was in order, and in the meantime he looked through the books.

Ben kept things up to date and carefully. His illness, which kept him sitting in an armchair with paralyzed legs for more than two years, allowed him to deal only with the ranch accounts, and these were well ordered.

From them Bud learned that there must be three thousand bulls in the pasture; twelve hundred cows and that the calf for the season had amounted to nine hundred calves. In the sales books, the last games from six months ago were listed. The last, of five hundred cattle, had been awarded to a cattle dealer in Nedles, California, at the rate of $ 48 per head.

That was what the books threw out. Now it was necessary to know what reality accused after two months of finding the ranching in the hands of Lowell and his team, and this had to be ventilated with that ganapán before giving him freedom of movement.

Fred announced that dinner was ready and when they went down to the dining room, the plates were already smoking on the table.

Bud invited the old cook to sit next to them and took the moment to question him about the affairs of the ranch. The details that Bill gave him, were not as to force him to dance with contentment.

Since Ben's death, two herds of cattle had been sold and had suffered a nightly robbery, due to a bold strike by cattle thieves. On the other hand, the expenses of the ranch in the hands of the inept foreman were excessive, and to cover them, he had sold part of the hay stored for the winter, which could cause a catastrophe if the natural pasture reserves were scarce due to bad weather conditions.

Regarding the team, everything he said about him was little to portray him. By saying that it was Lowell's making, it was all said.

Then he informed him of the general situation. The region was infested with cattle rustlers and rustlers. The Wilson Mountains served very well as a refuge for the outlaws and the town suffered under the rule of these, who were its true masters.

Bud was going to have a serious problem to renew his equipment. There were not many trustworthy people who could be counted on there and the few who could be useful and faithful, would not dare to accept the charges, because the continuous fight with the rustlers, meant a constant danger of death for them.

Bill offered to speak to two nephews he had on a farm in the county. They were both cow"boys, but they had resigned from such a dangerous position, employing themselves in agricultural work, less exposed, since the undesirables were more attracted to livestock than vegetables.

Bud thanked him for the offer and promised to pay them well for their work if they performed well. He needed to surround himself with tough and loyal people to fight the outlaws and he would start by setting an example of courage.

That night, fearing an unpleasant visit, not only by the cattle rustlers, but by the workers of the fired team, who might try to take advantage of the defenselessness of the cattle guarded only by Fred and Bud, they mounted a very severe guard; but the night passed without incident, and at dawn they retired to rest for a while, leaving Bill to watch.

In the middle of the day, Bud set out to campaign. His main concern was the renewal of the team. As long as he did not have suitable people, he would be tied hand and foot. Before leaving, he remembered Lowell and ordered:

"Fred, bring that bird, I want to speak a few words with him.

But to Fred's great surprise, the bird had taken flight. Smashing a window pane in the shed, he was able to file his bonds with the broken glass and escape, not without leaving a threatening note for Bud, in which he promised to take full revenge for the treatment he had received.

Bud was furious at the discovery. Now he could not say how many robberies had been committed on the ranch in the past two months and this would confuse the accounts.

But since the thing was hopeless, it was best to forget it, although it must not forget Lowell, who would become one of his most irreconcilable enemies.

After lunch, he went down to the town to meet with the sheriff, at whose orders he was going to place himself and from whom he was going to get the maximum help; but his visit to the first Whitebills authority could not have been more disappointing.

The sheriff, who was a man already hardened in the fight against the undesirables and who accused the traces of it with three scars that he wore on his body, welcomed Bud warmly, and when he had explained his mission in the ranch and his wishes , Told him:

"Look, Bud, I think whoever sent you here didn't like him well." In Ben's lifetime and when he was enjoying his powers and energies, he saw himself and wished himself to keep the undesirables at bay. Later, when he fell ill and had to rely on someone else's hands, his ranch became a nest for snakes, as Lowell, who was always lazy and spendthrift, took advantage of his lack of control to do whatever he wanted. with the help of his men, who were one of a kind. You have done a meritorious work sweeping away that leprosy; But do you think it will be easy for you to replace them with worthy people? The few that there are will not want to expose themselves to being "Colt" meat and the others will offer to join the team to help the cattle rustlers.The problem that presents itself is serious.

"Good, but is there no way to do something to clean up the region?"

"Yes, but where are the people capable of it?" I alone can do nothing and no one provides me with people for such a dangerous work. I'll tell you more: Among the several prominent cattlemen that infest this there is one, Ray Garson, who shortly before his death Ben "dented" five hundred head of cattle. Ray has not been shy about trumpeting it everywhere and I have not been able to stop him, because he surrounds himself with a few gunmen who would hardly have seen me approach him, they would have shot me. Ray frequents the town's gambling dens; he plays, drinks, gets drunk and when he runs out of a penny, he takes another hit where it seems best, and to live. Once I got several sheriffs in the region to gather a dozen and a half of their deputies to help me clean up and when I went to try, someone gave the tip, they disappeared into the mountain and there was no way to locate them. The assistants marched again bored and days later they shot me in the back that took me between life and death.

Now, if you feel more buoyant and gutsy than I do, I'm willing to give you the star, as long as you get what no one else here has.

Bud, who was listening carefully, replied:

"Very good, Mr. Oakle; I appreciate your reports and I will only tell you one thing: that ranch means something to me that is worth more than what they could give for it twenty times improved, and I have to defend it with hands and nails. I do not pride myself on being more than anyone, but I do affirm one thing: either I clean the region so that the business can prosper, or they will have to bury me here, and with that all my tribulations will be over. It all depends on me getting a trustworthy team together; if I succeed, someone is going to regret not having migrated to the other side of the Confederacy.

"That's the bone, Mr. Raines." Where is that team?

"Could you not address someone who feels guts to be part of it? My cook, the only decent person left there, has offered to speak to two of his nephews who work on a farm.

"Oh yeah! The Swansons, they're good guys, but they don't want to die so young.

"I'll see if I can convince you that it is easy to keep your life and do a good deed with me."

"Try it." For my part, I can point you to Jim Hopkins and Rufus Hanna. You will find the first one helping your father at the smithy, and the second one at Larry "el Bizco's" grain store. They are quieter professions than cowboy.

"I thank you for your reports; As for the rest, it may not take long for him to hear about me in the town. It is an obsession that I have to remind certain people of the saint of my name.

"Make sure you don't have to remember him sculpting him on a tombstone." It is very simple.

"And very difficult too." People say I was born with the "Colt" in hand. And it is funny that, pretending that I heal myself from this defect of living with the weapon between my fingers, they have sent me here, where you have to hold it in one hand while you drink the soup with the other.

Bud said goodbye to the sheriff, gathering the addresses of the four possible laborers for the ranch and marched in search of them, using all that remained of the afternoon to find them and convince them that they should support him in such worthy work.

But that night, when he returned to the ranch, he had the four grooms behind him, very happy to have a leader of such arrests.

CHAPTER VI

HOW YOU CAN GET 3,055 DOLLARS

The count of cattle in the pasture was quite heartbreaking. Of the 3,101 bulls, only 1,850 remained. The cows had been reduced to 601 and the calves by half.

Bud denied the plunder and swore by all that was sworn to rip Lowell's skin, if he was lucky enough to run into him one day.

After making a general visit to the ranch, he set about writing a report for Big. In it he gave an account of the reception they had received, the result of it, the lack of cattle and the pitiful state of the ranch and its dependencies, and after many studies he attached a budget of expenses to improve all that, which amounted to $ 2,501, which he begged to be sent to immediately undertake the works.

Bud's surprise and anger were enormous when he received a letter from Big in which, among other things, he said:

"I'm sorry I can't send you a single penny, but I'm not willing to waste money on something that I don't know yet if it's going to be worth remembering exists. I've sent you there with full powers to do whatever it takes. precise, but counting on the ranch's own means. I believed him to be an aggressive man, of ingenuity and resources to put things in order and make him prosper. To be the one to bear the expenses you indicate, I did not need to interest you in the business at fifty percent of the profits.

"Now, even exposing myself to losing them, all I can do is advance your pay for six months and then you with the job you want to give it."

When he read the letter to Fred, he screamed in the sky, railing against Big.

"But what does that old miser think, that you have the California mines on your fingers to get the chestnuts out of the fire?" What the hell is he offering you, if everything that can be returned to him if this is fixed, are you going to give it to him with your effort? And do you expect him to grant you the hand of his daughter? A horn! That usurer of the devil, what he's trying to do is get rid of you so that you don't marry her, don't you see that? And in the last extreme, if he does not get his way, it will be because you become a millionaire with your own danger, but without his help.

"What do you want me to do? Bud asked, discouraged.

"First, send him a letter sending him to hell." You must call him an exploiter, usurer, trickster and everything that comes to mind. Then you will tell him to keep that advance that you do not need it at all, and then not to think about showing up here one day, because as soon as he pokes his nose through these pastures, we will throw him into a pond with a cow tied around his neck.

"I can't do that, Fred," Bud objected. It's through Nancy.

"Don't say nonsense." Your duty is to do it so that he sees that you have more liver than him. Then we will see how we get out of this hornet's nest where we have gotten, and if you don't write to him like that, I swear to you that I left your mouth, with my fists, worse than I left it to Lowell.

Bud matured Fred's advice a lot; but he ended up realizing that he was right and he decided to write.

The letter was a model of a whip to scourge usurers. Without biting his tongue to tell him how much came to his imagination, he ended the letter, saying:

"Bud Raines has never asked for alms. You can save that advance, I don't want it, and I will or will not do what this demands, that's my account; but I warn you, if you happen to stick your nose in the ranch Before our contract is up, I'll throw him into a pond with the fattest cow I can find tied around his neck. "

That letter, which was supposed to revolt the rancher, closed off any possibility of carrying out his plans; But he was an aggressive man and he hoped to find some formula that would get him out of trouble.

The cattle, skinny and poor, could not be sold. To do so would have been insane, for all they would have given for each head was twenty or twenty-five dollars, and yet he needed money to clean up the ranch, pay for the peonage, and replace the pastures depleted by Lowell's greed.

All the money he had in his pocket was seventy dollars and five cents, and although Fred generously offered him the thirty-five he had, with that amount there was not even a week to support the laborers.

Bud needed to get money from somewhere, like he needed to augment his meager team, and he wondered how to get it.

Suddenly an inspiration came to his mind. Oakle had given him certain information that he had almost forgotten, and now, remembering it, he smiled wryly.

He checked his revolvers to make sure that they would work without reserve, and calling Fred, he asked:

"Listen to me, Fred." Would you like to be buried in the cemetery of this beautiful town? I have seen it and it is magnificent. It receives full sun and is quite well cared for.

Fred gave a sour wink and replied:

"I'm in no rush to be counted as a tenant in it." Why you ask?

"For knowing it." In that case, bye. I'll leave you in charge of the ranch, and if I don't come back, well ... well; Since you don't have any commitments, you can send him to hell.

Fred seized her by the arm and exclaimed furiously:

"Come here, you piece of ass." Where are you going?

"Do not worry. That is my thing.

"Listens. As you consider getting into a mess where you have to make a fuss and don't count on me, I swear you don't leave here, because I send you to sleep for a month with a punch.

"Do not bother yourself. There will be no brawl. There will be shots and census contenders from Whitebills Cemetery. That does not suit you.

"Well, that thing about me not going, let's leave it. I like punches better, but if there are those who digest lead better, why not give them that taste? What is it about?

"About two thousand five hundred dollars."

"Are you going to rob a ranch?

"No, but the sheriff has assured me that in a gambling den in this bucolic town for the excellent outlaw Ray Garson, who stole five hundred head of cattle from Ben." That figure, at fifty dollars, means twenty-five thousand. Ray plays hard at the gambling den, and he plays because he has gold from cattle raising. We need two thousand five hundred dollars and I have thought that the one obliged to supply it is Ray.

"Nothing but that crap money? No, sonny, I am not satisfied with that. You have to loosen the twenty-five thousand, plus the revenues, and if you don't, I'll beat your skin to the ground.

"Get rid of that idea, Fred." There will be no punches. There will be shots and fat. Ray is not alone; He is accompanied by three or four leading gunmen and they will have to shoot fast and well. Does it make you?

"Let's rehearse a bit." You know that I still don't shoot like you; But if you leave me the three or four gunmen and dedicate yourself to Ray, I think the thing can be resolved cleanly.

"Well, walk." Today is Saturday and the joint will be full. Let me start the question and don't look at Ray when I take part in the game. Take a look at his gunmen and shoot before you think about it.

"Agree. We're going over there.

Both of them went down to the town, not very crowded, but since it was home to rather dubious elements, always possessors of ill"gotten money, and cow"boys willing to expose their pay to win the gold, the gambling business was quite busy in Whitebills.

The important thing was to know where Ray stopped; but Rufus Harma cleared them of doubts, directing them to "The Gold Nugget", located in the main street.

When they both reached the dusty street and stopped in front of the establishment, they observed that it was quite busy. More than a dozen horses were locked next to the porch, and from inside came the muffled murmur of loud conversations, loud and rude laughter, the curses of some drunks, and the whole range of sounds typical of such an establishment.

Bud, his hand on his hip, pushed open the door and entered, followed by Fred, who seemed to be hiding behind him. The establishment was veiled by a thick smoke screen that made it difficult to distinguish the clientele.

Bud stood at the counter together, studying the topography of the land, and Fred surveyed the customers closest to the door.

Suddenly, he observed that one tip the brim of the hat forward and then left his seat, furtively gaining the door. As he did so, Fred remembered the features of the fugitive and, moving closer to Bud's ear, he said

"Don't do anything yet, wait for me." I am going to resolve an urgent matter; I'll be right back.

Bud tried to ask for explanations, but to no avail, for Fred had already won the fairway, disappearing swallowed by darkness.

Bud stiffened, wondering what business would have forced his friend to leave the tavern at such a critical moment; but, arming himself with patience, he waited.

Shortly after, an echo of a detonation came from outside, which although it forced everyone to turn their heads instinctively, it did not move anyone to go out to see what was happening and two minutes later Fred reappeared lighting his pipe.

"Where the hell have you gone? Bud asked quietly.

"To provide a nerve painkiller for a fellow who was a little unhinged." Fortunately I arrived on time and the poor man will no longer suffer from them.

"So ... that shot ..."

"It was the only painkiller I needed." It was one of the ranch peons, who, when he saw us come in, rushed out, no doubt to go in search of reinforcements and lay a trap for us. I saw him on time, followed him and ... before he had even thought of drawing the gun, I administered the dose. Now, you can start the dance whenever you want.

"Thanks, Fred." You are a wonderful man.

"And a horn! You tell me that, if you can, when this celebration ends. Ah! ... Regarding what you told me about the grave ..., if necessary, then make sure that the sun gives it good. You know that I am very cold.

"I'll have a stove installed, don't worry." Now pay attention.

He advanced smoothly through the establishment, until he reached a door that led to a large room reserved for gambling. There was a table with a roulette and, another, where the pharaoh was played, and the points made a good nucleus.

Bud didn't know Ray and had to find out who he was, but he hoped someone would call him by name, which would be enough.

Indeed, on the Pharaoh's table a tall and flexible individual, about forty-five years old, with steely eyes and rough, callused hands was carving. He wore two huge "Colts" on his belt that crashed into the table every time he moved, and he had a good quantity of gold coins in front of him.

Someone called to claim an unpaid bet, and Bud smiled. The banker was Ray and it was fortunate that he was, because given his posture at the table, he was in a poor position to draw his weapons quickly, perhaps because, trusting his poster of a terrible man, he did not even remotely suspect that someone could try something against him.

Bud didn't rush. He had discovered the outlaw,   but he needed to locate his guardians and this required certain study.

But it did not take long to discover some. Three individuals, more suspicious"looking than the rest, moved around the gunman, as if afraid that someone would reach out and take over the bench.

Bud took a look at this one. By the amount of coins stacked, he calculated that it exceeded the amount that he had indicated, and to avoid that it could diminish in some unfortunate move, he got ready to act.

He winked at Fred, who was hiding behind him, and I murmured:

"It seems to me that those three ...

"Do not follow; they have given me the stink. Worry about yours, I'll take care of those.

Sheltering himself in Bud's body, he extracted the revolvers, concealed them in the sleeves of his jacket, and maneuvered himself behind the three suspects' backs.

Then he smiled beatifically and sighed.

Bud, who had managed to make his way to the table occupying a strategic position, put a hand on the ledge and when the play that was pending was finished, he quickly drew his two revolvers, presented them at the table and shouted:

"One moment! I have something to say to Mr. Ray.

He tried to get up to draw the revolver, but Bud pointed it at his chest saying:

"Don't move, you can hurt yourself." They are from 45 ...

The outlaw, turning olive"colored, remained tense, but someone put his hands on his waist. However, they did not touch the weapons either, because a voice behind them shouted:

"Be careful, gentlemen, you are going to suffer from nephritis if you make a wrong move."

An enormous tension paralyzed all the breaths. The dots guessed something tragic was going to happen, but they had no idea what.

Bud softly exclaimed:

"Mr. Ray, a few months ago you saw fit to take from the" Cruz Alta "ranch, owned then by Mr. Ben, and today by his niece, Miss Nancy, five hundred head of cattle, which at fifty dollars adds up to twenty-five thousand. As this money belongs to that item and is the property of the person I represent, I am going to take it to account, and on another occasion, I will return in search of the rest.

Ray, amazed, was tense for a moment not knowing what decision to make. Of the many strange things that he hoped could happen to him in his life, this was the strangest of all, and his dull mentality could not find a way out for it.

But his self"respect as a man with a revolver on his belt, did not allow him that humiliation and, fast as lightning, he decided what he should do.

He materially sank into the seat to take cover on the table and steal the body from the bullets, being able to shoot from under the table, and he pushed it forward; But Bud, expecting something similar, took advantage of his standing and leaning forward to advance the revolver with his peculiar speed, and the shot hit the outlaw square in the head, without giving him time to fire. His three companions, disdaining the danger that Fred's presence posed to them, one of them threw themselves on him, ready to disarm him. Two consecutive shots cut off the action of the two closest, but the third had time to draw his weapon to fire.

Although the shot came from his revolver, it was too low, because Bud had been quick to target him as he watched his maneuver.

The three gunmen, fallen to the ground, scrambled trying to continue the fight; but Fred disarmed one with a kick and crushed the other's mouth, while Bud finished off with a shot at the third.

Panic seized the patrons, who rushed out of the gambling room, heading out to the tavern fearing that some stray bullet might find them in their path, and Bud and Fred found themselves masters of the room.

The gold had rolled on the floor when the table had been overturned by Ray, and Bud was scrupulous about taking more than what belonged to the bandit; But when he had to make a decision, he did a quick count of how much he could collect, $ 4,221 in all. The scoring points were relatively low and, doing a mental math, he left $ 1,221 on the table.

Then he looked into the tavern and exclaimed:

"Sirs, I don't want anything that doesn't belong to me." I leave 1,221 dollars for each one to take the position they had made. If anyone thinks something is missing, ask for it before we go.

Noting that no one was making up his mind, Fred stepped forward, inviting them:

"Please, one by one." You, how much had you put in?

"Five dollars.

"Like those. Other. You, how much?

"Seven dollars.

When everyone had marched, there was $ 55 left over. Fred, as if at an auction, asked:

"Make game! Is there no one missing to claim?

As no one protested, he kept the rest saying:

"Well, gentlemen, thank you very much." The rest is ours. Then, throwing ten dollars on the counter, he warned:

"For some wreaths of evergreens." It is used to the house.

And he walked purposefully towards the door.

Bud followed him with revolvers at the ready, and then, turning to the astonished crowd, said:

"Gentlemen, I have proposed to clean the region of mobs like this and I will succeed." I warn that I will do another raid when least expected. Now, if there are honest people left in this town and, above all, men who have two fingers of courage and dignity, in the "Cruz Alta" ranch, which I run, we need laborers to help me with that work. The one who feels alluded to, who shows up tomorrow to ask for a job.

And closing the door delicately, he went out into the street. Fred, who did not trust anyone, exclaimed:

"Hurry Bud, lest these people realize how easy it is to grab $ 3,155 and try to imitate us!"

And riding on horseback, they galloped away from the joint.

CHAPTER VII

FRED SANDERS LOVING TEMPERATURE

The next day, when Bud had not yet left the bed, he was very surprised to receive a visit from Fred.

"What the hell do you want, that you don't even let me rest when I'm comfortable?

"A pattern of your size should be the first to hit the navel. Don't you see me, ready to go down to the pastures?"

"Good, but it's you and not me who has to go down."

"Good, but you are the one who has to receive the visitors." Please get dressed and go down to the patio. There is a large committee of swallow children who want to talk to you.

Bud, very intrigued, threw himself off the bed, asking:

"Do you want to explain yourself, damn your stamp? Who are they and what do they want?

"They say they're cow"boys and they pretend to be part of the team."

Bud stared at him questioningly.

"What do you suspect, toad from hell? Do you think that they are types thrown by the cattle rustlers?

"I don't suspect anything." They seem to have the faces of good boys; But do not trust, that hell is sown with good intentions.

Bud hurried down to the patio, where eight young, stout, good"looking, laughing"faced boys stood stiffly waiting on horseback.

Bud examined them with a deep glance, being pleased with his picture and, approaching them, asked:

"What did you guys want?

One of them, assuming the representation of all, exclaimed in a broken voice:

"Well ... we came because ... they told us what you did last night in." "The Gold Nugget" and we wanted ...

Bud stepped forward, asking:

"Finish soon! Do you want to avenge Ray's death?

The cowboy raised his arms to heaven, exclaiming:

"God save us! We come because we have been told that you have asked for honest men and ... something brave, who are willing to help you and we ... maybe we can ...

"Basa! Do not continue, that if it costs you so much work to link a steer as to explain yourself, you are not going to serve me. It is true that I have said it. I need pawns to replace the rogues I kicked out of here, but I don't want rogues to replace the pawns. We're?

"We are decent people." You can inform yourself.

"Of course I will." You will leave me your names and I will ask the sheriff. If he answers me about you ... Fred, take their parentage and let them come back this afternoon.

Fred took the names and the boys left, apparently very happy.

"Looks like they're not outlaws," Bud suggested. This afternoon I will know.

Indeed, that afternoon he went down with the list to the sheriff's offices, who, as soon as he saw him enter, advanced towards him with outstretched hand, saying:

"Bravo, Mr. Raines! I congratulate you from the bottom of my heart. You have done something too big to admit without seeing. I believe that with Ray's death you have dealt a terrible blow to the cattle rustlers.

"You believe it? I estimate that now all those who are scattered around will get together and will try to give me the decisive battle. I have to be forewarned and for that I come to visit you.

"Tell me how I can help you."

"Eight boys have come to the ranch asking to join the team." They have given me their names and I want to make sure first that they are not suspicious people. Here is the list.

Oakle ran through the names and, handing him back the paper, said:

"I think you can accept them without concern." They're not suspicious, although I don't think they're all great cowboys.

"I do not care about that. They will learn. To teach them, even with fists, I have a foreman who is wonderful, giving lessons with his fists. The main thing is that you can trust them.

"Yes, and some boast of little men."

"Now, one last favor; I need a maid for the ranch, but I would prefer a rubble when it comes to beauty. I don't want to mess with skirts there.

"In that case I can recommend Ketty Grahan to you." She is a woman in her fifties, ugly as colic, but clean, hard"working, and agile. She lived with her brother, who has recently died, and needs to work.

"Well. Send her over there tomorrow.

Bud left the offices and, to take advantage of the time, visited various artists in the village. The carpenter, a painter, two bricklayers and a plumber. He was obstinate in getting the ranch clean up and remodeling quickly and didn't want to waste time.

In the afternoon the would"be laborers returned, they were admitted and sent to the pasture with Fred. This would be in charge of training them in the event that they need a lesson to begin to comply moderately.

That night, when the foreman returned from the pastures, tired of giving lessons to some of the rookie laborers, he went up to the room Bud had assigned him, and as he left the room, after changing his clothes, he stumbled on going out with Ketty. , the new maid.

Fred rubbed his eyes several times to convince himself that this was a woman and not a cover, and when he was sure of it, he ran like a madman to Bud's office, penetrating him like a whirlwind:

"Hey you; piece of ass! Is it that you want me to die of a fright?

"Because?

"But have you had the courage to hire that human wreck as a maid?" Have you ever believed that this is a circus? But what about aesthetics, Bud? ... And where have you left your sense of adornment and love of Fine Arts?

"Look, Fred, go to dinner and don't bother me." What did you want, for a fallen cabaret angel to hire you for your solace? No, sonny, formality must prevail here, or else everything will fall apart.

Fred, casting fire from his eyes, cried out:

"Those have us? Is it that because you are ostracized, you think that the rest of us are going to suffer the same evil? Well, you are wrong, I will prove it to you.

And very angry, he went down to the dining room, where the peons had already gathered, talkative and joyful, commenting on the day of his debut at the ranch.

For several days, the workers worked on the decoration of the hacienda at forced marches. Bud wanted to get this over with quickly so he could go about business without worry.

One night, shortly after the peonage from the pastures returned, a series of shrieks and reprimands came to his ears from the corridor, and when alarmed he left his chair to go out to investigate the cause, he burst into Ketty himself, the old maid, who, with wide eyes, gasping for breath and all choking, sought protection in him stammering

"Please, Mr. Raines, hold on to that madman."

"To who?

"To his foreman." Oh Mr. Raines! You don't know ... He's a savage ... and I ... I'm a decent woman ...

At that moment, Fred, very serious, with a face in which a flame of poppy remains seemed to burn, entered the office, saying very seriously:

"Come on, Ketty, don't be prudish." You know that I am madly in love with you, and I am a very important man on this ranch to despise my love.

Bud stared wide"eyed at him, not sure whether to burst out laughing or toss the inkwell at his head, but reacting, he pushed the frightened maid out into the hall, saying:

"Ignore her, Mrs. Ketty." Fred is very fond of playing pranks. You will get to know him.

"But ... he did mean to kiss me!"

"I do not doubt it. He told me that you remind him a lot of his poor grandmother, and that makes him sentimental.

The good lady left the office suspicious and Bud, facing Fred, exclaimed annoyed:

"Come on, Fred, you're too old for such jokes!"

"What jokes or what cooked berries! Love is blind! You are pushing me into the horrible abysses of antediluvian love, and I ...

"Get out of here, you phony! Bud yelled, threatening him. And listen to me well; As you try those tricks again to make that unhappy woman leave the post, I swear to you that I will look for another one that is older and more horrible, to see if you really die of fright.

"It's okay. Is that your challenge? Well I accept it.

And he left with dignity, laughing to himself at the bad time he had put the unhappy maid through.

Days later, the ranch had been transformed. Cleanliness and adornment had replaced dirt and neglect. The walls were white as salt mines, the door jambs painted green, the railing also painted and renovated with pots and plants that it had never had. The windows had curtains; the beds, new clothes, and furniture had acquired a new patina, thanks to the varnish used on it.

Bud had had one of the rooms with south windows painted light green. A nice cheery walnut bed with all the new equipment had been installed in it, as well as a pine sink, side table, and beveled moon cabinet. A mosquito net covered the bed to protect midsummer nights from parasites.

Bud had reserved this important reform, but Fred, prying into what had been done, found him shocked.

"Have you become a damsel from the East to reserve this birria room? He asked in amazement.

Bud, blushing, yelled:

"Shut up, snooper from hell! I do not have to give you explanations.

"It's what I needed to see! Fred grumbled. A man who claims to have come into the world with the "Colt" in his hand, afraid of mosquitoes! ... Where have you hidden the compact and the lipstick?

"Do you want to shut up and go to hell?

"I don't feel like it, and right now you tell me and I'm leaving! I serve whole men, not half, ladies.

Desperately Bud reached out with his fist and dropped it on Fred's forehead. He scrambled, hitting him straight to the chest, and the two of them hit each other down the hall, until they ended up in Bud's office, where he fell onto the couch with a good punch.

"To hell with you! Fred roared. The bill, right now!

"Go away, or I'll shoot you and I'll destroy you, you piece of ass! Have you not understood that I have prepared that room for the day I get married?

Fred burst out laughing, saying:

"Who are you planning to marry, with that witch you brought as a maid? That's why you felt jealous that I made love to her. As it is not with that one, I predict that you will not marry ...

He couldn't finish the sentence. She had to get out on her feet, slamming the door shut to avoid catching the inkwell Bud had thrown at her from across the table.

Fred did not appear before Bud for two days. When he returned from the pastures, he would dine with the peons and then quietly retreat to his room without exchanging a word with his friend.

But this one did not pay attention to him. He had more important things to attend to, and he knew that his overseer's anger was more feigned than real, no doubt to try to worry him.

Bud suffered from various obsessions, which were the ones that kept him awake. One was the possible acquisition of some land adjacent to the ranch, which could bring him various profits. Another, to increase his pastures in proportion that would allow him to have a greater number of cattle without worries; then ensure water for them, because a magnificent stream ran through it that one day they could dispute if someone went ahead to acquire the land and, finally, protect their cattle much better, since the strip of land had a natural barrier of rough slopes, that would serve to cut there the possible action of the cattle rustlers.

The other obsession went hand in hand with this one, since both could complement each other. It was that, during one of his long horseback rides around his farm, he had discovered among the canyons, canyons and ravines of the nearby mountains, some horses in the wild, and it was said that, if he managed to capture and tame them , the profit that its sale provided, could be used to acquire the neighboring land and expand the number of cattle, suddenly giving greater value to the farm, without having to disburse money that he did not have, or wait months and months to that the business alone would yield that problematic utility to expand the business.

Bud had kept the discovery for himself and did not want to report it to his foreman until he had all the data necessary for a successful endeavor. If there really was a good herd of wild stallions, he wanted to convince himself of it, study the places they frequented, observe the terrain only to render that problematic utility to broaden ready, proceed to capture them.

This work consumed him many hours of browsing and observation, until one day he returned to the ranch in triumph. He knew everything he needed and thought the company was easy enough. He had discovered that the horses were going down to drink in a pool enclosed between cliffs. This redoubt had a narrow exit to the East and the entrance on the opposite side. If the exit was closed and they were harassed by the entrance, they would be left locked in a large natural corral, where linking them would not be a human thing.

The day he finished his observations was Saturday and when, late at night, he returned to the ranch, he decided to call Fred and give him an account of his project.

He was sure that the finicky foreman would be delighted at the discovery and, having a great passion for horses, would be an enthusiastic aid in their capture and taming.

But when he sent for Fred, they told him that he had dressed in long shots and had gone down to the village together with the team.

Bud, in a bad mood, resigned himself to putting off his plans until Monday. He could not force his foreman to live in constant vigil on the ranch and gave him the right to have fun like any man at his command.

He took the time to mature his plans, drew a sketch of the terrain, marking the place of the trap, where it should be closed and the place where they should be stationed to harass the herd, and, tired, retired to sleep.

Sunday was boringly spent horseback riding and went to bed relatively early, looking forward to Monday for the exciting hunt.

That night, and late at night, the cook, who was sleeping in a shed near the palisade, awoke with a start when he heard the door being banged violently and, taking his revolver, as Bud had ordered him, he went to the door. and, before opening, he asked:

"Who goes?

"Open now, lame from the devil! Cried Fred's scruffy voice. Do you not know the right arm of the emperor of this ranch?

Bill was a little startled when he heard Fred. It was the first time he had observed him drunk, but he was quick to carry out the order.

When he opened the door, he was deeply astonished. Someone else was riding on Fred's horse, and judging by the shapes, it was a woman.

Fred put the horse into the yard and, dismounting, exclaimed:

"Wait a bit, Queen of the West, now I'm going to prepare a lodging for you worthy of your royalty."

Bill stared at the Amazon and made a dismayed gesture. She was a young and highly painted girl, wearing an outfit of the most frivolous one can give herself, and the peon did not hesitate to classify her among the adventurers who served in the gambling dens of the town to brighten the life of the peons.

Fred took her in his arms, dismounting her like a feather and, linking her around the waist, said:

"Come this way, you piece of heaven." We're going to surprise the bearded ogre on this damn ranch and show him that Fred Sanders also has an exquisite taste for choosing maidens. Tonight you are going to sleep in the most regal room in this palace ... That's it!

Bill tried to get in the way, but Fred angrily yelled:

"Get out of here, lame devil, or I'll give you a shot that will spoil the other oar!

Bill gave up before his attitude, and Fred, dragging the girl who seemed a little puzzled, made her climb the stairs, until she reached the upper floor, where Fred had his bedroom.

He stopped at Bud's door and, pounding on her fiercely, yelled:

"Jew from hell, get up and open up, I'm going to give you the biggest surprise of your life!

Bud awoke with a start at Fred's pounding and screaming and, pulling on his pants, went out into the hall.

The young man was left as one who sees visions when confronted with Fred, who was forced to lean against the walls to keep his balance, and even more when he observed the girl, who was looking at him with wide eyes.

Bud, furious, turned to his foreman, yelling:

"But have you gone crazy, Fred?"

"Mad? Yes of course. Crazy of love. Do you see it? What do you have to say about this angel in an evening gown? You do not like? What is more beautiful than that grotesque that you have brought us to make our eyes bitter? Well, take a good look at it, but nothing more, because it is for me alone. That's it ... I'm going to install her here like a princess for my only recess and right now you're going to give me the key to that empty golden cage that you have, because for who better than for an angel like this?

Bud, beside himself, advanced towards him with clenched fists and roared:

"What I'm going to give you is a punch in that toad mouth you have so you can learn to drink."

"To me? Try and see how ...

He didn't have time to say more. Bud reached out with his fist, catching Fred on the chin, who collapsed like a bundle.

The girl gave a cry of horror; but Bud reassured her, saying:

"Don't be alarmed, nothing's wrong. It is the only thing she needed to make her sleep those dreams of loving greatness that have suddenly entered her, and as for you, I am very sorry, but I cannot welcome you in this ranch. There are only men here who have enough of their temperament not to need stimulants.

She protested in distress at the mockery of which she had been subjected; but Bud, inflexible, pushed her towards the stairs and calling Bill, ordered:

"Here, Bill, give this young lady those five dollars to console her for the trip and put it gently on the fence gate."

Bill obeyed the order despite her protests, and when he left her on the other side of the door, he went to sleep, wondering what would happen the next day when he was confronted with the foreman, free of the fumes of the foreman. alcohol.

Bud didn't care about his foreman. He dropped him where he was and retired to his room, giving himself up to sleep.

When he got up very early, he was still there, and taking a bucket of very cold water from the patio basin, he threw it into his face without any contemplation, forcing him to jump like a dock.

Fred, dripping with water, shivering with shock and wide"eyed in surprise, stared at Bud, not understanding what was happening, until, reacting, he became enraged and shouted:

"What are you doing, you piece of ass? What do you think I am? Some thirsty frog?

"What you are is a drunkard without shame, and on my ranch I don't want drunkards." Get ready and go preparing your luggage, you get out of here.

There was such seriousness in Bud's face that Fred, alarmed, exclaimed:

"But Bud, have you gone crazy?" What have I done to you to make you treat me like this?

"What have you done to me? Do you think I can tolerate last night?

"But what was last night?"

"Don't you remember that you came drunk as a barrel, wearing an angel from I don't know what hell on the back and you tried to accommodate him in nothing more than in my golden chamber, as you call my private room?

Fred looked at him stunned and stammered:

"Did I do that, Bud? Swear to me I have! But I did believe that I had been dreaming that ...

"Stop it! If you want to set up a harem, find yourself a gambling den in the town, and you will be the queen there. Not here.

Fred was devastated. He no longer remembered the soaking or realized that he was shivering like a newborn dog.

"Oh, Bud! He exclaimed. I swear I don't know anything about what you tell me. You don't understand, of course. A man is a man. You have to alternate when the occasion arises. Anyone can drink one more glass. Then love ... You are an anchorite for that, but I ..., I am a man and ...

"Go to hell, you bad beast! Bud yelled, realizing that if he went on like this for long, he was going to get pneumonia.

"""Well; since you want it, be it. I will go. My only regret is leaving you alone for the world ... Who is going to shake your chamois better and more elegantly than me?

"And who is going to shoot your mouth but me, if it takes a long time to disappear from my sight? Bud yelled, pushing him down the stairs.

"Well, okay, ogre." Well, you do not presume little because they have given you the parody of a ranch! If at the end of the day you are going to get what I ...

"You go? Bud yelled, beside himself.

"Yes, man, yes, I'm going." But you will come looking for me and you will not find me. I'm the best foreman in the whole West, even if you don't want to. Ah! ... and the most handsome. You have already seen it. Women are raffled on me. Instead, you ... you only know how to fire shots and kill gunmen. Bah! A life like yours sucks!

Bud tugged at one of his boots and threw it at his head; but Fred dodged the blow and descended shivering and laughing at his companion's fits of bad temper.

CHAPTER VIII

TWENTY-FIVE CORN

Fred ignored Bud's order, and went to the pasture, sure that he would pass that black time, and Bud was glad of it, because deep down he did not hold a grudge against Fred, knowing that he was not a man. fond of drink.

In the evening, when he returned, he went directly to Bud's office, and very seriously said:

"Well, old friend; I hope that you have passed the basca and that you have forgiven me for that last night. Now I swear to you that it was something unforeseen and that it will not happen again.

"It's okay. I want to believe that it is so and I take it for granted. Now listen. Tomorrow morning I need the eight best pawns to ride. I have something on my hands that is formidable.

"What is it about? Asked Fred, intrigued.

"From hunting at very little cost, two dozen magnificent wild horses."

"By hell! Is that really, Bud?

"As I tell you.

"Well, tell me about your discovery." That's great, Bud!

He realized how much he had been observing, and showed him the plan he had drawn for the hunt. Fred, eyes blazing, studied him.

"Good, boy," he said. If you catch those two dozen stallions, you've been saved. When they are tamed, they can be worth twelve thousand dollars very well.

"I have calculated that and with that money we will buy the pastures adjacent to ours, ensuring water for the summer.

"Good thinking, Bud." It seems to me that we are going to hit that old miser with the poker on the knuckles.

"Let's not do projects, Fred needs to have the horses."

"We will." But first you have to secure the trap. Let me close the exit to my liking.

Fred marched the next day to the location Bud had indicated and surveyed the terrain. The young man had not been mistaken and the trap could be magnificent.

With the help of two laborers, he cut down a few stout trees that he nailed to the ground, then traversed thinner ones. Furthermore, he took some pieces of wire from the warehouses and lined the gaps, and finally, he fabricated brackets that secured the trap against an attempted rupture by holding it from the outside.

Two days later, Bud, Fred, and eight peons left the ranch before dawn and took up positions in order to circle the terrain where the horses were to appear. Well hidden and positioning themselves in favor of the air so as not to be discovered by the fine noses of the stallions, they waited patiently with the ties tied to the saddles.

About eleven o'clock in the morning, a beautiful specimen appeared, white as snow. He announced their arrival by clanging his mighty hooves on the shale and they all rushed to cover the heads of their mounts so they would not be denounced.

The horse reached the end of a ramp and stood like a statue, scanned the air uneasily, but it said nothing because the pawns had positioned themselves in such a way that he could not carry their scent to him.

Quiet, it seems, he released a high"pitched neigh that echoed like the vibrating of a bugle through the hollows of the cliffs and, shortly after, the galloping of a herd hammered on the slate of the path like an approaching thunder, until, They appeared in a heap, jostling each other furiously and scanning the air uneasily.

Bud and Fred, who were staying together, exchanged silent admiration at the sight of them. They were all magnificent and there were black, like night, bay, white, white, painted, with whimsical spots and of various elevations.

Bud had to bite his lip to keep still and not maneuver ahead of time, while Fred, lasso in hand, peeked out from behind a rock, following the stallions' path.

"Twenty-five! He murmured. One more of the account.

The animals descended to the other side of the ramp and headed down some trails towards the pond. This was in a small ravine and, ahead, a narrow gorge led to the trap that they had prepared to corner them.

Bud waited for them to enter the ravine, the other exits of which were taken by the peons, and when everyone was inside, he launched his horse into a gallop, followed by Fred's and fired a shot into the air as a signal for the peons to maneuver.

The shot revolted the stallions. His boss stretched out his ears, whinnied loudly in anger, and turned his back, trying to escape, but when confronted with Bud and Fred, he swerved around and looked for another way out.

As they searched for the gaps in the gorge, pawns who prodded them appeared before them and the animals, maddened, finding no free exit other than the gorge, threw themselves tumultuously through it, while the pawns followed them to avoid the retreat But the white horse, sensing a danger, turned fiercely and when he saw Bud and Fred in the middle of the glen, he darted towards them, trying to pass them.

Bud, realizing it, prepared his lasso and in a magnificent effort managed to lock him by the neck, but this was not enough and the stallion, powerful, tugged on the lasso as he was about to yank Bud out of the saddle.

The rider spurred his horse trying to make him run at the gallop of the stallion, which was not possible and he would have had to let go, if Fred's opportune lasso had not fallen on him, reinforcing the prey.

The noble brute defended himself like a beast for more than a quarter of an hour, but, finally defeated, frothing from his mouth and lips and with bloody eyes, he stood still, as if resigned to his fate.

Better locked, he was taken to the gorge where the peons, mad with joy; They had cornered the entire herd and were closing the fence with powerful tree trunks that had already been laid out the day before. The confinement had been splendid and now it only remained to lock them one by one, find a suitable place for them and proceed with their training.

As no one had heard of that magnificent hunt, they were not in danger of being robbed, but for greater security, two laborers guarded the trap night and day, while the others, in free hours, working at night and leaving it reduced to the minimum. The custody of the cattle essential, they built two large barracks to house them based on sturdy tree trunks, impossible to knock down.

With great precautions they were transferred to their new confinement and once there, Bud, tirelessly, dedicated himself to tame them with the help of Fred, who as many moments as he had free, as many others went to the barracks, in search of a horse to accustom him to the bite, the saddle and the spur It was not a lazy task, but neither was it very long. They all became docile after half a dozen attempts to fit the saddle and the bit, and only the white stallion was tough at dressage, making Bud sweat like he had never sweated in his life.

But, little by little, he gave way in his savagery, until he ended up being the most docile and noble of all.

When he was satisfied with the result, he said to Fred:

"I had twenty-four and there were twenty-five." I will give this one to Nancy so she can be proud to ride it.

"But you won't do it before the wedding, will you?" Fred asked. Be careful, what happens to someone who gives bread to someone else's dog ...

Bud didn't answer; but she decided to think about when she was going to make the gift.

At the moment he had no intention of doing so. Old Big had given no more signs of life after that insulting letter and he was not going to be the one to stoop to explaining his actions.

The voice of the magnificent hunt carried out, spread through the village, to Bud's great annoyance, who felt uneasy about it, and more than one onlooker peeked through the pastures to take a look and appreciate the beautiful sheet of so exceptional horses.

This had Bud on fire. He wanted to have them completely tamed to get rid of them, for his heart told him that they were going to try something to strip him of his treasure.

The two most determined pawns on the team stood guard day and night, and both he and Fred assisted them in this task until late at night; but, despite this, a lively restlessness dominated them.

Two days later, the sky was cloudy and, as the afternoon progressed, the clouds, thicker, threatened with water.

Bud, restless, called Fred and said:

"Tonight we will reinforce the guard in the sheds and we will stay as well." I fear that this is the one they will take advantage of to attempt a daring coup.

Four pawns remained on guard. One outside and three inside, plus Bud and Fred, who had armed themselves to the teeth.

The darkness was so dense that the watchman could not see ten feet away and, although he made an effort opening his eyes, he only saw before him a black veil that blotted out everything. It was late at night when the peon braced himself with the revolver. He had seemed to catch a touch that was slowly approaching and he was restless and uneasy.

Nervous, he thought backing up and going into the sheds to sound the alarm; but not wanting to leave the entrance unguarded, he hesitated for a moment and, finally, even exposing himself to being mocked, he pricked up his ears, fixed his gaze on the place where he thought he perceived the touch, and fired.

Undoubtedly luck helped him, for the shot was followed by a hoarse cry of pain, and immediately several detonations came from various places, but around the sheds.

The pawn, with one leap, won the door, and lying face down on the ground, fired trying to prevent the shed from being attacked, while Bud, Fred and the rest of the pawns emerged with rifles in hand, nervously asking what it happened.

The pawn warned:

"Don't go out." I felt someone crawl and fired. I must have hurt him, for he groaned. There must be many and they surround the sheds.

They spread out, as best they could, and through the hollows of the trees they fired at random or guided by the glare of the attackers' flashes, since the density of the shadows did not allow to fix the target. It was a blind fight that went on for a long time. A bullet, filtering through the clearings, put a pawn out of combat, but the besieged must have managed to bring down an enemy, for they had caught roars of pain and staccato curses.

Bud was furious at not being able to distinguish his attackers or even attempt an exit against them and, in case he lacked something to feel uneasy, the horses, terrified by the roar of weapons, were agitating terribly in their stalls, threatening to break the obstacles and cause them a terrible conflict.

Finally, the vague line of dawn was marked in the blackness of the sky, and the shadows, partly lightened, allowed the besieged to distinguish some bundles that were preparing to flee when they saw their surprise plan failed.

Bud, impetuous, did not resign himself to letting them go without discovering who they were, and haranguing his men, exclaimed:

"Whoever wants to follow me." These rustlers must be taught a lesson so that they lose the desire to repeat the play.

Riding on horseback, he launched himself into the valley followed by his men, and the "rustlers", surprised by this unexpected departure, separated, trying to disappear into the nearby mountains.

But the fury of his attackers partially thwarted his plan. Some managed to escape the harassment and disappear among the rugged mountains, but four bit the dust without time to flee.

Bud had pounced on one of the fugitives, drawn by his black"spotted chestnut horse. He wanted to remember where he had seen that strange mount; But, failing to do so, he thought that by shooting down the rider he would clear up doubts, and although he was about to be the victim, since the fugitive shot very well, he managed to place a shot in the back that threw him from the horse, remaining stuck in the land like a toad.

When she reached him and turned him to examine his face, she gave a cry of wild joy:

"Lowell! ... Ah, damn scorpion, I finally managed to pay off the debt you owed me!

When he was reunited with his men and a search was verified, four corpses stared up at the sky with their glazed eyes. They were all from the old ranch team, and this detail allowed them to presume that Lowell was the one organizing the attack.

They also found near the sheds the body of the other robber who had been shot down by the pawn, and Fred, scratching his head, muttered

"Make ten bucks, Bud."

"So that? Asked the latter, puzzled.

"For another five crowns." You already know that we have established that custom and we must not miss it. Two dollars for each toad of these is not a bad price, Bud would gladly pay two full months to be able to apply it to as many jackals of this species.

"Okay, here," Bud said, handing him the money, "but they're getting ruinous for me." From now on I lower the rate to one dollar.

"Don't be nasty, Bud." Don't you understand that if they find out that you are so mean in that last tribute they will feel disgusted and they will not want to get within range of our rifles? If in the end your troublesome father"in"law is going to pay for it!

Bud didn't want to argue any further and retired to the sheds, where they proceeded to calm the stallions, which took a lot of work.

A week later, Bud closed a deal with a rancher in Las Vegas, Nevada, and gave up the wild stallions at the marked price of $ 12,111, reserving only the white horse, which he had baptized with the challenging name of "Hurricane." .

When he found himself the owner of the money, he negotiated with the State to purchase the land adjacent to his pastures, and part of the remaining remainder was used to acquire a point of yearlings, which one day soon would increase the value of the property by quite a bit. percent.

Although Bud believed Big hundreds of leagues away from knowing the truth of his maneuvers and his combinations to fulfill the terms of the contract and, above all, to give his "troublesome father"in"law" a lesson in ingenuity, daring and aggressiveness, the truth was that Big was up"to"date with everything Bud was doing, since he was in close friendship with the sheriff of Whitebills, who took care to keep him up to date on everything that was happening at the ranch, sending him a weekly letter that Bud did not even have the knowledge of. most remote suspicion.

And so he learned, as well as of the settlement of the ranch, of the death of the outlaw Ray, of the rescue of those three thousand dollars that had been so useful to him in saving the first anguished pothole that presented himself, and, later, of his fate. and cunning discovering the herd of stallions and capturing them, as lately from the sale of these and the acquisition of more pasture land and new cattle to add to the depleted flock.

Big rubbed his hands in delight as he watched Bud's aggressiveness and tenacity, but he kept quiet and reserved for her news. He believed him so vain that he would not hesitate to rub his face with the success obtained with the capture of the horses and the sale of them; But the days passed and Bud was still as tight as the mountains that enclosed the Grand Canyon.

CHAPTER IX

AS A BUD BALANCE A PENDING ACCOUNT

One morning Big, furious, called his daughter and showing her a letter he had just received from Oakle, the sheriff, said:

"What do you think of that fool? After not deigning to write a word or give an account in the more than four months that he has been at the ranch, he dedicates himself to walking like a king with that magnificent white stallion that has been reserved, as if he really were the owner of everything and we cast aside as a despicable thing. Do you think that should be allowed?

Nancy, who had been on fire for a while longing for Bud's absence, replied:

"It's your fault, Dad." You have treated him like the last pawn on your ranch. You sent him to a company in which he has risked his life dozens of times, improved the ranch, acquired land, cattle, etc., all without helping him a penny, and now you complain because he reserves his successes. What have you done to make him behave differently?

"I had to cut your flights, Nancy." You know it. He is a terrible man and if I give him wings one day he comes and says that this ranch also belongs to him.

"It seems to me that you judge him very superficially." I believe that all this is nothing more than secondary education. Bud is a sentimental romantic at heart.

"So romantic that he makes love to the daughters of rich ranchers and tries to rebuild his fortune by that means."

"No nonsense, Dad." You are earning what will be yours.

"Yours? As long as he doesn't get on his knees before me, crawling, I think he's going to be left with the desire.

"You have a signed contract with him."

"We'll see how it has been accomplished at the end of the year." I'm afraid it falls short.

"We'll see. I think it will be long.

"You are another romantic, who only see in him the heroic and conceited man, whose successes shine with the "Colt" in hand. For now, as I am tired of the treatment you give me, I am going to write you a letter that is going to burn your hair.

"Be careful not to answer with another one that burns your mustache and you don't know how to answer it. For my part, I will tell you that I am tired of this annoying situation and that I need it to be clarified once and for all.

"Well, well, I'll clear it up, and today."

And, indeed, that very day he wrote Bud a letter that was going to be like a tinderbox.

The letter Bud had to go over twice to convince himself of its content read like this:

"Dear Sir:

"Four months ago I placed excessive confidence in you, entrusting you with the administration of my daughter Nancy's ranch, and this is the date that you have not yet rendered the slightest account of the profits, nor have you consulted me in the smallest detail about what to do or not to do, according to my daughter's interests.

"As this conduct is not correct, I hope that as soon as possible you will send me a statement of accounts and a list of your activities to improve the property, which I very much doubt you have achieved, since your silence is too eloquent in that sense.

"Lou Big."

Bud erupted in a storm of cursing at the tricky old rancher and, without pausing to think further, took up his pen and replied with the following letter:

"Dear Sir:

"I cannot say, gallantly, that I was surprised by the tone of your letter, because it is the only thing I could expect from you, after your previous date four months ago.

"You ask me for a statement of accounts and, as it is my duty to give them to you, here you have them:

"For the salary of 14 laborers for four months, at $ 61 a month   3,361

"For the foreman's salary for four months, at $ 81 a month   321

"For my manager's salary for four months, at the rate of 100

dollars a month ....
400

"For a four"month salary to an assistant, at $ 20 a month   80

"For the maintenance of 16 people for four months, at a rate of

16 dollars per day ....
          1,920

"For spending 25 crowns, at $ 11 per crown, for as many

 enemies of his property, whom I killed with exposure of my life ... 250

"Total dollars   6,330

"As apparently his fundamental concern is to pay off this debt, understanding that its amount will be very necessary to meet the needs of the ranch, I include this extract, sure that by the fastest means available to him he will send me said amount .

"You could add other small expenses "the projectiles spent against the enemy cattle of your property "but these can wait for the final balance.

"In returning the affectionate greetings that you send me, on behalf of all of you, I remain your servant,

"Bud Ruines."

* * *

When Fred heard of this hurtful correspondence that night, he was outraged to the point of paroxysm at Big's vileness, but laughed out loud at the harsh and well"deserved reply.

"That's good, Bud." And I think you should add that if from this day our salary does not increase, we will go to another less stingy ranch.

"Leave it as it is, it is already served. With this letter there are only two attitudes: either to come in person to discuss the matter or to burst and swallow the content.

Bud was right, because when Big got the letter, he was genuinely outraged and yelped that scared his own daughter.

"But do you think this is tolerable, Nancy?" This is an insult to your father, which I cannot consent to.

"What did you want me to send you the gold from the California mines?

"No! ... But it did give me a true statement of accounts and not cheating. Where is all that the ranch has yielded and why am I not aware of it?

"You know where it is: Oakle specified it for you." He has bought new land, he has bought more cattle, he has fixed the ranch. All of that is there. Instead, what have you given him for the peremptory expenses? Nothing he has done has been done with our money.

"What about the money you rescued from Ray? And the one who has produced the sale of the horses? Is it that you have used everything in what you specify?

"Possibly not; Had he done so, he would no longer have a team, no foreman, or maid, because no one works without pay. It is true that he has hidden those earnings from you, that they do not really belong to the ranch, but he must have made it annoying for your attitude. In his day, when he fulfills the contract, they will come out.

"   Sure! You have to defend him, what are you going to do? You are more interested than me ... And this tagline that adds to the balance? Fifty dollars for crowns to the dead! ... Is it believed that I am a philanthropic burial society, that I must crown everyone who dies in that damned town?

"Of course not, bolt keep in mind that he refers to the undesirables that he has had to eliminate to defend our property.

"I'd like to see it ... Fifty dollars! ... Twenty-five crowns!" But, is it that it is believed that I am going to steal the money to satisfy his craving as a man hungry for blood like hyenas? For me, let him kill them; But let him put in his grave a bouquet of wild flowers, which are within reach and cost nothing. How luxurious and looked the gun"man is coming out of me!

Nancy, very amused by her father's indignation, asked:

"What do you plan to answer?

"What I intend to answer I reserve." In your day you will know.

"Well, I hope you don't die of a stroke with the answer."

"I hope so too." Instead he may have to meditate for a long time.

Big insisted on not giving details of what he was planning to do, and Nancy, very amused by Bud's reply, prepared to leave him, not without warning:

"Well, as courteous does not prevent bravery, when you write you send my regards." I don't think there is any reason not to send them to you.

"No, deep down, maybe not, but in the way ... Well, I'll see what I do."

When Big was left alone he smirked. Although he had shown himself with such outrage, this was nothing more than a mask. He was liking Bud's energy and, above all, his demonstrated ingenuity in getting out of the bad trance he had put him into and the real value he was placing on the ranch.

But he wanted to humiliate him and make him suffer before giving him his daughter, and this he believed he would achieve at little cost.

Following Bud's departure, he had hired, on the recommendation of a friend, a new foreman. This was a tall, strong, fat, and tough young man, who must have possessed unusual strength, and this was going to be the one in charge of bringing the answer to Bud.

He called the foreman to his office and, after an examination to convince himself that his projects could not fail, asked:

"Tell me, William, would you like to earn a hundred dollars?"

"   Gee, boss, you don't even wonder!

"Good, but I must warn you that you are not going to win it for just going to a rodeo."

"I can imagine it; but I hope it is something that I can develop.

"Judging by his palm, I think so." It's about giving a certain guy a good beating.

"Nothing more than that?

"Nothing more. It is well understood that there should be no fireworks game. The thing must be with a clean fist, and if in addition to the beating you manage to bring him across the saddle of his horse, I will add a hundred dollars to the offer.

"For that price I carry it on your shoulders." Who is it about?

"From my former foreman, Bud Raines, who now runs my daughter's ranch in Whitebills."

"Well, I don't think it's very difficult to beat him with your fists, but you forget that Bud was born with the" Colt "in his hand and that if he takes to drawing, then ...

"""It is not accurate. You must present yourself unarmed. Tell him you're in charge of beating him up and bringing him to the ranch and you won't get out of this program. Rest assured that then, and under no circumstances, Bud will be such a coward that he shoots at you.

"Very well. Well, immediately I go there. I urge to have those dollars in my pocket as soon as possible.

* * *

Bud spent a few restless days, wondering what Big's reaction would be after his letter and what he would do when he was treated like this.

She wasn't concerned about the old rancher's attitude, or what he thought of him, but she was concerned about what his attitude might influence Nancy's spirits. His silence had broken her heart and she wondered if she was influenced by her father to stop any closer relations or if, indeed, both would try to make fun of him, believing him an inept incapable of carrying out the arduous and dangerous work that had been done. tax.

The morning of the first Sunday, from the date on which he sent his aggressive letter, brought for him an unexpected response and an even less expected surprise.

Fred, who hadn't made up his mind to go down to the town, fearful of losing his equanimity and relapsing again with another love scene like the one from the night of yore, was in the yard going over some chaps, when he caught the trot of a horse that left. He was approaching, and, surprised by a possible visit, he abandoned his work and looked curiously at the gate of the fence.

An imposing"looking rider stopped before her and, without dismounting, asked:

"Is this the "Cruz Alta" ranch?

"It seems so, friend." What can I do for you?

"Is Mr. Raines in it?

"Depending on what it is for."

"I have a personal assignment from Mr. Big."

Fred curiously examined the guest who, strangely, had no weapon on his belt and asked:

"Any letter by chance? "

"Not. The commission is personal.

"And non"transferable? Fred asked sarcastically.

William, for he was the newcomer, looked him up and down with contempt and replied:

"As much as that, no." I can pass it on to you, but after you've tried to give it to Mr. Bud, if he isn't in a position to receive it.

Fred caught the threatening air of the reply and, guessing a trick, replied:

"It smells to me that you are coming to eat the children raw, and if so, I'm afraid your teeth are still too milky for it." Anyway, everything is received here and everything is returned ... even with revenues. Will you keep the revolver in storage until after you've discussed the matter with Mr. Bud?

"Are you afraid of being killed?

"No, it's for your own personal safety." You could trust him too much and ...

"I have no weapons." You can register me.

"   Bravo! You only come armed with fists. I really admire your guts. I would like the boss to give me the pleasure of talking with you later.

"If that is your wish, I offer myself to it with or without permission from your employer."

"Very grateful, though ..."

"What?

"Nothing. That I am afraid I will not make it to the banquet on time. Wait a bit, I'm going to let you know.

Fred, very amused, went up to the office where Bud worked and, putting his hand on the book, warned:

"Put down your pen and put on your shoes." Down there you have a messenger from Big's ranch.

"What do you have, a letter? Bud asked, getting to his feet quickly.

"No, sonny; but bring a pair of fists capable of knocking down a six"year"old bull.

"What do you mean by that, Fred?

"That he should bring the order to answer your letter with his fists." He comes without weapons, a sign that Big has lectured him on how dangerous it would be to deal with you with "Colt" in hand; but, instead, he is boastful and aggressive, speaking of personal assignments transferable to me, if you are not able to take care of them.

Amused, Bud did a few push"ups with his muscular arms and, lighting his pipe, descended into the courtyard, where the Herculean William was curiously awaiting Bud's presence.

This, phlegmatic, addressed him saying:

"Good morning friend. I am told that you have a certain very personal assignment for me from Mr. Big.

"That's how it is.

"Well. Well you will say.

"The job is simply to give you a good beating in response to the tone of a certain letter you sent him and then carry it across the saddle."

"Nothing more?

"Nothing more than that."

"They paid you in advance for the work, didn't they?"

"No, but that doesn't bother me."

"I do, because it will be a pity if you come back with a handful of teeth less and then they deny you the twenty dollars that that miser will have offered you, with which you would not even have to renew your teeth."

"That's not your account." So I await your orders to beat you up when you are willing to.

"For my part, we can start right now." I was just looking forward to doing a little exercise that would make me want to eat ... Do you think this site is good?

"I'm indifferent to him."

"Me too. He warned you in case you find the patio tiles too hard for your head to bear ...

"Do you think yours will withstand the blow?

"I haven't bothered to think about it." I do not intend to test the harshness of its content.

"We'll see that. Anytime you like, Mr. Bud.

"You can start when you like, sir ..."

"William, my name is William Polk."

"Okay, write down the name, Fred." You will need it for the judicial registry and to order the usual crown from him.

"Wow, another two bucks on the bill!" Big is going to be ruined at this rate.

Bud braced himself for one of the roughest seizures he had ever suffered. He did not disdain the strength of his enemy, nor the rough and thick fists he displayed, and the confidence he displayed in success. William must be a professional fighter used to dealing with tough men, and while he also relied on his fists and the skillful lessons that Fred, his teacher, had given him, he knew he would have to put his whole soul into the fight if he didn't want to see each other. exposed to that brute conscientiously fulfilling the order they had given him.

Trusting all the success to his flexibility of legs and waist, in what he knew would be better than his rival, he began the fight with some threats to the face without intention of carrying them out and only to orient himself on his rival's fighting capacity and tactics that he was going to use.

Soon he was convinced that he had only in front of him a big and strong man, hard of fists, resistant for the punishment and blind for the punch; but he lacked any school to dodge and break the guard of his opponent, and this reassured him.

He would let him get tired forcing him to use too much mobility for his weight and when he had broken him he would dedicate himself to being the attacker, with all the aggressiveness and liveliness that he possessed.

Within ten minutes of the fight, William was panting like a hunted steer. Bud had forced him to use too much of his legs and arms with very little performance, and he was realizing that it was not as easy to defeat this flexible foe as he had calculated.

It was true that he had managed to touch Bud's face a couple of times, making him bleed from one ear and had even applied a regular blow to his shoulder without receiving the slightest caress, but that was not enough and he needed to apply his strength to him fully. fist somewhere vital on your body.

He was looking for a way to smash his face or put a fist in his stomach, when at a signal from Fred, who was calmly witnessing the combat, Bud rushed to the inn and, before his enemy had had time to anticipate the attack, had received a huge direct in the mouth that forced him to spit blood mixed with a few curses from the best cowboy lexicon.

Fred, who had begun a gesture of approval at the magnificent blow, warned:

"Careful, Bud;" leave a tooth in its place so that I have later where I can distract myself. The gentleman has gallantly promised me to practice a little while with me when I put you out of action and if you apply another direct one like that I will not find more than the lot.

William, biting his lip, roared:

"I'm going to undo you both, you filthy pigs!" You still haven't seen what a man like me is capable of with his fists.

“Not; We have not seen it ... nor will we see it and it will be a real shame ... for you.

The overseer, furious at these jabs, tried, in a desperate attack, to break Bud's guard by stepping onto his ground. The young man, with a jump, dodged the tactic and his right fist was nailed in an eye of his opponent, who raised his hands to protect his face, immediately receiving another blow to the stomach, which forced him to bend forward to fit. a third from the bottom up, crushing his nose horribly.

The cowboy, bruised, in pain, blinded by blood and enraged by the beating, lost his composure and blindly, as if his arms were mill blades moving mechanically, he threw himself at Bud in an absurd way, presenting his face to the blows that the other wanted to administer, without succeeding in applying a definitive one.

And so, in five minutes, he was knocked out with his face completely swollen.

One last blow, applied to the chin without any obstacle, sent him to sleep for a few hours, and when he found his body on the ground, Bud, who was sweating like a damned and could no longer hold his arms from the weight he felt on them, he wiped the sweat from his forehead, exclaiming:

"What a piece of elephant! I thought I was not going to end him in my life!

"Yeah, it was a bone, Bud," Fred said.

"But it has been very useful for you to deal with him." You have to bear in mind that many of those can fall on you, and you have to be trained to deal with them.

"Whoa! The first of these mastodon to boast of bravo again I cut the race with shots. I was born with the "Colt" in hand, and that is my strength.

"Well, dear." What do we do now with this toad?

"What? ... Wait, I'll tell you right away. Go preparing your horse and his.

Bud went up to his office and wrote a short letter which he put in an envelope, then went down to the patio and said to Fred:

"Kindly cross him in the saddle and ride your horse." Put that letter in his pocket and walk him to the door of Big's ranch. I want to be sure that he and the letter reach their destination.

Fred curled his lip at the command and exclaimed:

"Hey, what have I done to you to apply that punishment to me?" Have you noticed that from here to Grand Canyon it is a little over a hundred miles in a straight line?

"As if there were two thousand." I want you to see how I have put your gunman so that he does not tell you a lie and think about it a bit before repeating the test.

Fred, resigned, tied his hands and feet to the foreman in case he reacted on the road and grumbling made his preparations to leave.

CHAPTER X

BIG URDE A TOO DANGEROUS PROJECT

Several days later Big was in the company of his daughter leaning over the railing of the ranch contemplating the landscape beautified by a beautiful sunset, when the rancher, fixing his gaze on the valley, towards the path that led to the ranch, exclaimed extending arm:

"What the hell is that moving around there? It looks like a horse without a saddle.

Nancy followed the direction of her father's arm with her eyes and replied:

"It seems. It is a horse that must carry something on its back. I see like a sack hanging by the flanks.

They waited, full of curiosity, until the horse, which was advancing at a good pace, was drawn, with more precision. It was then that Big, amazed, added:

"   By the horns of a cow! If what you carry is a man crossed on the chair.

She swiftly descended from the railing down into the courtyard, and when she opened the fence gate, the horse had already stopped beside her.

Big recognized then the mount of William, his foreman, and as he approached the bundle pierced on the back, he did not need to look at his face to understand that he was his envoy.

But when he tried to make sure of this, he suffered a shudder of horror as he observed how the mayoral presented a bruised and swollen face, all full of blood, as well as his clothes.

Enraged, he broke into loud shouts asking for the wounded to be taken care of and helped by the cook and another cut his ligatures and transferred him to a bed, where they proceeded to carry out an emergency cure.

William, although he had regained consciousness on the way, lost it again because of the pain and the terrible posture he was carrying on the horse and thus, when they put him on the bed, he was an inert mass that was not in a position to give the slightest reference to what happened.

The peon proceeded to undress him and, in doing so, discovered among his clothes a letter addressed to the rancher, which he hastened to deliver.

Big, yellow from the bile he was swallowing, tore open the envelope and read:

"Mr. Big:

"I never supposed that you were so vile, that to pay off your legal debts you used thugs by trade, and even less that you reserved your face like men.

"You have sent me a bear from the Black Mountains so that instead of paying me the $ 6,311, he would give me a beating worth that amount; but you have priced me far below my strength and I hope that from now on you will give them a beating. fairer value.

"I am giving you back your human steamroller because it has not served me well. If you really want someone to eliminate me, send me half a dozen like that, if the matter has to be solved with fists, or half a dozen gunmen if we must solve it with shots .

"I thought I had given it back to him a little more presentable, because I understand that the poor man will arrive in a mess, but I did not dare to do it, because the budget of arnica and iodine was going to be excessive to add to the bill, and I am not willing to do more advances.

"And now, know this: Either you pay off what you legally owe, or I will seek a mortgage on the ranch; whose interests will go at your expense. I am your industrial partner and you are the capitalist, and therefore it is up to you to contribute money for general expenses.

"Waiting for your quick reply, greets you,

"Bud Raines."

Big unleashed a terrible storm of epithets about Bud and his family tree, from Adam to the present day, but Nancy, who had been amused by the letter, cut off his verbiage by warning:

"Dad, I already told you that you were risking another disappointment." You have thought yourself stronger than Bud and you are breaking your knuckles against the iron when you pound on him.

"No, damn her spirit!" Big roared. I have not believed any of that. What I try is to cut the fumes and at the time to test his mettle, but it is proving too hard for me and that is my fear.

"Because? Did you need a damsel to run the ranch business? Weren't you convinced that there was only a need for a man like Bud?

"Yes, and I don't complain about it, but I do complain about the lack of respect with which you treat me." He must have realized that I am going to be his future father"in"law and that I deserve more consideration than he gives me.

"Which ones have you given him? You reap what you have sown, and listen to me well: as it takes a long time to solve this matter, I am afraid that in the end it will not have any solution.

"Give me the formula if you think it's so easy."

"Me? Have I perhaps put together this Tiberium to have to undo it? That you, you have made a formidable mess. For my part, I'll only tell you one thing. Although it bothers you, I am very happy about what is happening. Bud has behaved as he should in this matter and has done what no one else would have done in his place to save this and give me back a fruitful ranch from what was a hornet's nest. I think the time is coming to clear up these misunderstandings and put things in their true place, because I fear that at the last minute I will judge the same as you and all the loving house of cards that I have raised will come to the ground without justification and for my misfortune.

Big got very angry with his daughter for those words. She was nothing more than a selfish one, who instead of thanking him for what he had tried to cut Bud's nails and turn him into a sensible and rational being, she was doing his part to encourage him and allow him to continue to turn into a beast.

They were discussing the matter heatedly when the cook announced the visit of Laurence Raft, the rancher.

Nancy angrily got up from her seat saying:

"You greet him, Dad." I'm that guy through and through.

Big, eager to annoy her, said:

"Well, not me." I have realized that he is the ideal man for you and I am regretting that I gave wings to that other guy to woo you. I think you should think about it a bit and study the situation. Raft is a rich man, kind, understanding ...

"And silly and ridiculous," she exclaimed excitedly. The man who woos a woman, who surprises another by kissing her and who after allowing himself to be spanked by him insists on courting that woman, has no dignity.

Big, maliciously, replied:

"What do you know about that? Do you think that if Raft were to meet Bud again to dispute your affection, he was going to let himself be so stupidly defeated? Well no. I'm sure it would make his face mush and cut off the bully fumes he has forever.

"Who, Raft? She asked dismissively. I would bet my soul that no.

"Yes? Well, I make you a proposition, to show you that your idol has feet of clay.

"Which? Nancy asked defiantly.

"I know what is coming." He continues madly in love with you and is insisting every day that I accept him, in principle, as an in"law son, so that he can make love to you without restrictions. I am going to propose that he remove Bud from your path and then I will have no problem in giving him my fullest authorization to make love to you officially.

Nancy laughed nervously and replied:

"And you think it's so stupid that I accept it?

"Why not? You misjudge Laurence. He's a very brave boy ...

"You think? Well ... I accept. Let him try going to the ranch to get what that bear William hasn't gotten, and if he has the guts for it, and he comes back victorious, I'll resign myself; but it is well understood that if he returns it to you in particles, I do not want you to blame me.

"Don't worry, nothing like that will happen." Laurence will be the man who knows how to avenge the humiliations that that rude guy has inflicted on me and who makes it clear who he really is a man.

Nancy, shrugging, left her father's office. She was so convinced that Raft would not only fail, but would take a terrible beating, that she did not think about the commitment she had made in the remote event that Laurence succeeded in defeating Bud.

Big gave the order to bring Raft in. The dashing and handsome man, wearing a very elegant and explosive outfit that made him the western cowboy dandy, entered the office resolute and determined.

Big looked him over from head to toe doubtfully. He wasn't a bad guy; He proved to be strong and hard"built, but next to William he was a featherweight, and yet Bud had beaten the strong foreman beautifully. But Big, who was a psychologist and in addition to a sneaky and mischievous character, had very different projects from the ones he had exposed to his daughter.

She did not reject Bud, nor did she hold any grudge against him other than the one she felt was so proud and indomitable. For the rest, he admired his qualities: wit, aggressiveness and pride, and believed him an estimable future son"in"law.

But there was something else about this that he wanted to liquidate without exposing himself to being branded as a variable man and not very firm in his convictions.

Long ago, before Bud emerged as a meteor in the ranch's history, Big had half"compromised with Laurence's father to harmonize a possible bond between their children. It seemed that this was a business for both and something very useful sentimentally for all, because it would unite the two fortunes and make the couple an ideal marriage.

Big did not hesitate to accept the idea in principle, especially considering that of the young men who could stand out in Grand Canyon there were very few who could meet the conditions desired by him for his daughter, but he took good care to leave her safe. Nancy's will, the one she couldn't force for something as serious as marriage.

At first, he found Raft nice and friendly, but gradually he began to dislike him. He was too presumptuous, a little fickle, more a friend to bragging at parties and rodeos than to hammering his bones into the saddle of the horse and linking cattle to mark them, and he told himself that this was not fit for a rancher in his school.

The pastures must be cared for and guarded by their owner and if not, neither the laborers work with faith, nor the cattle are safe, because the cattle ranchers always find an open gap to cut the barbed wire when they know that the master's eye does not keep the ranch.

If something could be missing to not feel convinced of the young man, it was highlighted by the scene in the patio the night that Bud administered that sovereign beating and the little dignity shown later, by continuing to be in love with Nancy and willing to marry her despite of knowing that another man had crossed her path with the possibility of success, committing an action that, not being repudiated by her, left him in a ridiculous place.

Big welcomed Laurence warmly, asking:

"What's up, dear Raft? Where do you walk so gracefully at this time of the afternoon?

"Only to see you, Mr. Big."

"Oh, for me not having bothered to waste a couple of hours in front of the mirror. We cattlemen are better off the more we smell of beef.

"Yes," Raft smiled, "but even though I am coming to see you, I am not coming to see you ..."

"Understood. That justifies a lot of things. Well, my dear friend, what do you bring against me?

Laurence coughed to clear his voice a bit and said:

"Well, really, to insist close to you on something we've already talked about a few times, but this time in a more serious way." This morning I exchanged impressions with my father and he encouraged me to come and talk to him, recalling certain conversations that you two had some time ago.

"Now! ... I remember that we talked something about certain extremes, but you will understand that I have only my will, but not that of my daughter.

"Of course, of course! But you are heavy.

"Eighty"five pounds more or less," said the rancher seriously.

"I mean, your advice weighs heavily." If you show interest in it ... maybe Nancy will make up her mind and ...

Big launched into the full attack and replied:

"Listen, Laurence." I have remembered my conversations with your father and have tried to incline Nancy's spirits towards you. At one point, I thought it was decided, but something unforeseen came up and ...

"I know what you mean," Raft interrupted, grimacing, "but that seems to have happened." Fortunately for him, Bud was absent and Nancy doesn't seem to have taken his absence very seriously.

"Not precisely your absence, but you already know women, especially those from the West; They are impressionable, they fall in love with virile and brave men, they admire them for their aura of unbeatable men and they let their love incline to admiration rather than to the feeling of affection itself. My daughter is no exception, and I can't swear that Bud hasn't left any imprints on her spirit. However, something has come up that puts the situation in a tense moment and perhaps someone who knows how to take advantage of it can take a great advantage of that terrible gunman.

"Not that gunman, not so terrible, Mr. Big." Such a man there are dozens of them in the West.

"You better put it on me then." The fact is, as you are not unaware, Nancy has inherited a ranch in Whitebills, whose ranch was a hedgehog, there was no way to reach her without pricking her quills. I sent Bud there with the healthy intention of pricking himself, but he must have been skilled enough to rid his skin of the caress of the quills, and this has caused him to grow to such a degree that he has become rude and unbearable.

"He does not show signs of life, he does not account for his actions and when, annoyed, I sent him a letter on behalf of my daughter ordering him to fulfill his obligation, he replied so rudely that Nancy has gone through the roof and justly.

"To punish him, I decided to send one of my pawns, the one who promised to give him a good beating, but ... you know what paid people are. He took it with little heat and ... the result has been that instead of spanking the sheepskin, he has been spanked.

"I cannot tolerate this state of affairs and I have decided to go to the ranch, to take care of it, but, I suspect that things will not be that easy. I am already many years old and neither my agility nor my resistance are to face them. with a bold young man, but I have no choice but to expose myself. Nancy does not want to and is so desperate, that I positively know that if a man with guts emerged capable of giving him a good beating and lowering the fumes, oh, that man would have a lot of cattle to win her love.

Big had craftily reached the desired point. The balloon had been launched and all that remained was for that young man, conceited and foolish, to pick it up.

So it was. Raft, with fiery eyes and a gesture of unbearable pride, got up saying:

"When do you want us to go to the ranch to settle this matter?

Big pretended to be surprised and said:

"No, no, Raft! I don't want to expose you to failure. It would hurt me if this were to serve as a pretext for you to lose the ground that you have gained in my daughter's heart. Think that if you were defeated in these climactic moments, she would despise you for having made her conceive hopes that she cannot really acquire.

"Well, I appreciate your interest, but I know that I have no other path shorter and more straight than that." On the other hand, I have a debt to pay to Bud and I am infinitely happy that this opportunity presents itself to allow me to pay it off and, at the same time, take away what can hurt him the most in the world. I am determined and I will go.

 "Well, I don't want you to believe that I want to take away the slightest chance of getting what you deserve, but I insist that the test is very dangerous for you."

"And I appreciate your insinuations, but I think I'm sure of the triumph." Do not forget that where there is one man another arises.

"That is very true."

"So I hope you'll tell me when the march is."

"Well ... let's say three days from now." I still have some preparations to make.

"Well, I'm happy and I'll come here." Now, if you'll allow me, I'm going to have a chat with Nancy.

"I think you are at a bad time today." Nancy is in a terrible headache because of that man's letter and you will understand how annoying it would be for her to talk about things unrelated to her situation. I think you, would leave it for tomorrow, I take it for granted.

"Well, if you think so, I don't insist."

Raft said goodbye to Big, promising to satisfy his desire for revenge and retired very happy from the opportunity that had been presented to him to decide Nancy. His outstanding debt to Bud must be satisfied, and he was not a man to forget offenses of that nature.

On the other hand, Nancy's love was well worth the sacrifice, and he was in love with the girl as passionately as Bud could be.

CHAPTER XI

A PARTY INTERRUPTED

Maliciously overjoyed, Big began making preparations for the trip to Whitebills. On that trip, he was going to leave many interesting things resolved, although he was also aware that he was going to have an interview that was too sour with that powder of his representative, whose nerves and pride there was no one in the world capable of breaking.

What was most difficult for him was convincing his daughter to accompany him. Nancy was looking forward to being with Bud again, but after everything that had happened she was scared of the first meeting, which could backfire, if Bud was as angry with her as he had with his father.

Big wasted all the eloquence he was capable of convincing her. If the young woman really loved Bud, if she was willing to get rid of Raft's assiduities and discard Raft from her path, and if she wanted that nervous tension between Bud and them to dissipate, she should agree to the trip, because if someone was needed Let him act like a diplomat, no one better suited than her to overcome Bud's stubbornness.

This outraged Nancy and she replied:

"What's your idea now, dad? That I save you from that ridiculous posture that you have adopted for your own pleasure?

The rancher scratched his head, puzzled, and replied:

"Well, maybe you're right about that." I do not feel very comfortable in relation to him, but you must not forget that everything I have done has been in defense of your interests and to stimulate on the one hand and pull the reins on the other to that wild colt, wilder than all the stallions he has hunted in the mountains.

"All that is very good, but with it, you only show me that all the good things you have as a rancher you have horrible as a politician. I'm going to have to bear the brunt of the brawl if I don't want to throw my relationship with Bud out of the window, and in case something was missing, now I'm also going to bear the responsibility for what happens to that cretin Raft.

"10h! ... Not that. For the record, I have fully warned you of the risk you run in feeling like a hero. If they send you to the dentist because of you, go ahead.

"All of that, counting on Bud spanking him." Have you thought about what would happen otherwise?

"Of course it is, but that ... would not be a serious thing."

"How not? It would be hard for me to break up with Bud for good, because it would be unworthy to see him humiliated by that puppet. You would have to compensate him, God knows how, for all that he has done on the ranch and you would leave me betrothed to Raft, who would demand, and rightly so, that I marry him.

"Not that! I have only promised to consent to him officially besieging you. What I couldn't assure him was that you would marry him.

"I wouldn't have missed more than that." Anyway, you've done a bad job. You take Raft to the slaughterhouse as it is vulgarly said and that is not very noble.

"Well, it won't be, but don't you think he's earned it?" He keeps harassing me and harassing you and somehow I have to charge it.

"Have you not thought that due to the hatred they profess, they can settle this question with gunshots?

"Wow, that is not! But I won't allow it.

It would be too much. I'll talk to Raft and warn him that I don't want shots. You wouldn't want him with bloodstained hands.

"Tell him I will not love him in any way and he will be more noble."

"That never. That moment has passed.

Nancy was about to say that she would, but, realizing the upheaval it was going to cause her, she refrained.

To make the trip less onerous, Big had his gig ready and, for convenience, he had one of the laborers accompany him on horseback, who had the gray jackfruit tied by his bridle that Nancy used to ride on her daily walks.

Nancy planned to go alone with her father to the ranch, but at the last minute she had to agree to the requests of Rosa, her maid, who, although she said nothing of the real reason that made her long for this trip, felt inclined towards Fred and I was also looking forward to seeing him again.

One morning, the procession started, to which was added Raft. It seemed that he was going to conquer the New World and if he did not lead an army of scouts to give him an escort, it must have been because their numbers did not give of themselves that much.

Very proud and proud, he kept his horse to one side of the gig and his smiles were like a flourish dedicated to sowing roses on the young woman's path.

This, serious and self"absorbed, had her thinking much further away than Raft supposed. Nancy, distraught, wondered how Bud would welcome them and what situation they would both be in for the future.

But Laurence, conceited and proud, believed that the girl cared only about the outcome of her next fight with Bud and even dared to insinuate:

"Don't worry about it anymore, Nancy, you'll see how everything is resolved to your satisfaction and without violence."

She looked at him indefinitely. He had always thought of him as a being endowed with very few lights, but he had never assumed him so frivolous and unconscious and he told himself in his heart that a new and definitive beating was very well earned so that he would learn to judge the things of life with a little more realism and humanity.

This thought made her give up her intention to speak with him and force him to renounce an action that was not going to bring her anything beneficial. Everyone had to enjoy what was well earned and Raft had no right to earn more than what he himself was looking for.

* * *

It was the middle of October. Autumn was already announcing itself, slowly stripping the trees of their bright green finery and in the distance of the rocky peaks the snow was beginning to weave its shroud, announcing that it would soon spread it across the valley. In the mornings, the water in the ponds appeared with a thin patina of ice that the sun was able to melt immediately, and, at night, some logs burning in the hearth were appreciated.

Bud was turning twenty-four that day. Bud had forgotten until the day he came into the world, but Fred was kind enough to remind him with no other encouragement than to annoy him by making him see that he was walking old.

Bud heeded the warning and arranged an extraordinary meal for his laborers that day. She would eat with them in the general shed, present them with a large apple pie that the old maid had made with care, after the meal she would give them a few glasses of brandy and some cigars that she had acquired in the village, and even present them with some. songs of his harvest, to the beat of a new guitar that he had acquired to vent his moments of melancholy, when the memory of Nancy overflowed in his soul and he needed to remember the beautiful decisive night of his life, singing the old song that thus changed the course of its existence.

The cowboys, warned by Fred, who knew everything, had decided to return the treat by giving him something practical and together they had acquired a magnificent "Colt", with a bone grip, on which the name of the favored person was engraved.

The revolver had been carefully stored in a wooden box, wrapped in cotton bubbles and tied with silk ribbons, as if it were something subtle and delicate.

Consequently, Bud had decreed that this day be considered a holiday, and except for a couple of laborers who watched the pasture and took turns every two hours so that everyone enjoyed the party, no one worked that day.

After the meal and when it was time for the toasts, Fred got up with the glass in his hand and, demanding silence, placed the box delicately on the table and said:

"It feels very bad to me that these beasts of pawns in my charge have commissioned me to be precisely the one who gives thanks for the party and congratulates Bud Raines on his birthday, and I say that it tastes very bad, because I am a man so not easy to speak, that I am afraid I can spoil such a beautiful act.

"But, finally, this ass and I have fought so many times that even if we do it again today, it would have nothing special and it may even turn out to be the most appropriate as a worthy end of the celebration.

"Dear Bud, I have the task of these good boys to put in your hands a small gift that they have acquired together and dedicate it to you as a symbol of your struggles and your efforts for the prosperity of the ranch. If they had left it to my whim, I swear to you that instead of this thing that is enclosed there I would have given you some garters or a corset, because I understand that it is what suits you best, given your withdrawn character, your native shyness and your lack of courage to ride a horse, swallow you in the saddle five hundred miles, to sneak into the ranch of that creeping Jew called Lou Big and bring his daughter Nancy on the rump, which is what your ancestors and mine would have done had they lived in this age, in which we all boast of being brave and in the end,We are just tame donkeys who have learned to handle a revolver quickly, as we might have learned to handle a sickle or a rake.

"But, well, as the thing is hopeless, here I give you the gift and I, for my part, will be wondering when you will be ready to use it so that people do not forget that you were born with a Colt "In your hand since apparently you have fallen asleep, with the weight of the weapon.

And for the record, if you allow us to do so, the graceful will take your place and we will throw you into the pond like a mangy frog, so that you die of disgust under the silt. I think I said what I had to say.

A round of applause greeted the incongruous speech, and Bud, who had listened to him between amusement and annoyance, rose, glass in hand, saying:

"Gentlemen, the speech of this Fred beast has moved me in such a way that I don't know whether to shoot him five times in the belly so that he can digest well or give him a hug, because of the interest he takes in me."

"You cannot criticize people on the day they turn twenty-four, without having married, when the one who does it has already turned twenty-five ...

"I protest! Fred exclaimed. You are insidious. You are accumulating years for me and that is playing with an advantage.

"I insist on what I said and I will keep it with my fists if the aforementioned shows me that I am lying. On the other hand, I am the most interested in fulfilling such a beautiful program, but things have not been as easy as this ass thinks. In any case, to prove it to you, I am going to fulfill what is being asked of me with such haste. Before a month I will go to the Grand Canyon to look for Miss Nancy and I will bring her here by degree or by force, but if later the whole region of Colorado burns in shots I will make those who get lost be found by this barbarian who believes that love is like cattle, which can be stolen by the strongest.

The applause cut off the speech and Bud, intrigued, untied the package until he discovered the revolver.

He took it in his hand, examined it with pleasure and leaving it in the box, exclaimed:

"Thank you very much, friends, but ... I would like to ask God to only serve me to decorate my office and not to test its quality on the meats of a fellow man." Life changes people's feelings and I, who thought I was born only to live with the "Colt" in my hand, today I feel as Fred said very well, who seems to me to be asleep from the weight of the weapon.

"When in an unforeseen way I learned one night that it is easier to win the love and heart of a woman with the strumming of a guitar and a song born from the bottom of the soul, I have acquired the conviction that it is not with the revolver that the that you can get the most beautiful things in the world, but destroy them.

Fred scratched his head at the argument and replied:

"Well, you may be right, but if you don't get it ... you can keep it, which is the interesting thing."

Someone showed up at the shed with the guitar for Bud to sing a song, as everyone had a great interest in it, and while Bud was indulging them, Fred left the meeting to take a look at the pastures. But as soon as he had left the fence, he returned like a soul that the devil carries screaming:

"Bud! ... Bud! ... They're coming! They are coming!

The young man, hearing him and believing that it was some new attempted assault, called for the revolver and with it in hand he went out into the courtyard followed by his men, asking:

"Who is coming? Damn your figure, spoilers!

"Who is it going to be? Fred replied nervously. That Big Jew. And it does not come alone. With him is Miss Nancy and that puppet Laurence Raft.

All the joy that had caused him to hear that Nancy was coming was embittered when Laurence was named, and, wistfully putting the revolver in its holster, he murmured:

"Well. It is seen that my good intentions are useless. Someone has written in the book of my life that I have to die with the "Colt" in hand and they will succeed.

He crossed the yard and stepped outside the fence, taking a wide look at the path that led to the ranch.

Kicking up clouds of dense dust, the gig moved toward him. From the slope he could perfectly encompass Big's figure, thick and satisfied, with his hands crossed on his stomach and a malicious smile on his lips, while Nancy, serious and severe, with her eyes fixed on the road, seemed more worried and anxious. How pleased with that visit.

Beside him, haughty on the horse, covered in dust but upright as a pole, Laurence walked, and Bud thought he had never found Nancy so beautiful, nor had he ever found Laurence so ridiculous and unsympathetic as he did that day.

Pawns lined the doorway in two rows to greet the coveted mistress, and Bud, biting his lip in excitement and anger, stepped forward a little, but never far enough to make them believe he was going to pay homage to the travelers.

The gig stopped by the fence and Laurence, diligently dismounting from the horse, came forward to extend his hand to Nancy to help her down, but she pretended not to see the gesture and did so from the opposite side, leaving him disgruntled.

Bud caught the gesture and thanked it intimately. He had had a wild urge to rush to the carriage and plunge his fearless enemy into it.

Mr. Big, who had descended first, stepped forward to Bud saying:

"Good afternoon, Mr. Raines." I want to assume that you would not expect this pleasant visit.

"I cannot object to your assuming what you want," was the dry reply.

Nancy, after a brief hesitation, stepped forward and extended her white hand to him, exclaimed:

"Good afternoon, Bud, how are you?"

`` Very good, Miss Nancy. I am not asking you, because I can see that you are perfectly fine. Do you want to honor me by going inside?

He beckoned to Fred, who was gawking at Rosa, Nancy's maid, and ordered:

"Fred, what are you doing standing there?" Guide these gentlemen to the rooms above.

Big, observing the lined up pawns, was surprised at the case and asked:

"What the hell does this mean? Did you have news of our arrival and have you mobilized all these gangsters to guard your back?

"I don't need it yet, Mr. Big." Today they are celebrating.

"Party why?

"Because it's my birthday and I've invited you to eat in an extraordinary way, giving you freedom for the rest of the day."

Big pretended to be shocked by such an act of lavishness and grumbled:

"How? But do you think that I pay the team to take advantage of any pretext and stop working?

"When you decide to pay them sometime, deduct from my salary the amount that corresponds to them today. In the meantime, don't brag about what you haven't done yet.

Big bit his lip and replied:

"Well, we'll talk about that."

Fred, who had lost all his poise when confronting Rosa, ran over several of his companions while trying to guide the travelers and marched ahead, while Bud, turning his back on Laurence, who had been staring at him with spiteful eyes, he followed Nancy leaving him insultingly abandoned.

Raft jumped up in front of him saying:

"Hey, Bud." You can be a great gunman, but you can also be polite. I have been accompanying Mr. Big and the least he has had to do is say good afternoon and invite me in. The rest can come later.

Bud looked him up and down and replied:

"I am in the habit of greeting whoever I like and not doing it with people I don't like." If you come with Mr. Big, let him be the one to invite you in. I am not at his service, but his.

Big turned quickly and, linking Laurence by the arm, said:

"Excuse me, Raft, I was distracted by the discussion." Of course you are my guest and, therefore, as the ranch belongs to my daughter, which is as much as being mine, I am the one who invites you to come in on her behalf.

Raft seemed satisfied with the moral slap given to Bud and entered on the rancher's arm, while Nancy, deliberately staying behind, shortened her step until Bud was beside her.

He suffered all the pains of purgatory, not knowing how to behave with her. Nancy seemed cold and worried, but she was the only one who had gently tried to break the ice of this situation, that she could not stay in such a position for long.

Nancy stated:

"I find the ranch very changed, Bud." It seems that renovations have been made in it.

Bud ceremoniously replied:

"Yes, something has been done to clean it up, although in truth I assure you that I did not expect you to honor him so soon with your visit." If I had known, I would have made the arrangements extreme ... if it had been possible for me.

"Much has been done to him." I remember it from when I came to see my poor aunt four years ago and it was a shame. Why didn't you tell us?

"Miss Nancy, there are many things that I have not said and not because of lack of desire, but because my opportunities have been cut off. I hope that one has come to speak and then you will know many things that you do not know.

They had reached the top of the floor and Bud stepped forward to guide them to the office.

They all entered him and Bud, standing up, asked:

"Do you have a preconceived plan, Mr. Big, or do you leave it up to me?"

"I bring many, but they can wait." What do you propose?

"If you're interested in having us visit the property first."

"Well, let's visit her."

Bud led them through, showing them around the interior, which had been redone and looked cheerful and attractive.

Big, with a serious face, did not comment on anything, but in his heart he was pleased with what he saw.

When looking out to the gallery; Nancy looked at this one full of pots that were beginning to wither and exclaimed:

"Oh how nice! In summer this gallery must be ideal!

"It's not bad." Now the vines are beginning to grow that will provide shade and it will be better.

He had left for last place to show them the beautiful room destined for Nancy. When he opened the door and showed him, Big exclaimed wryly:

"I see you lead a foodie rather than a rancher's life, Mr. Raines." This room is more like a woman than a man.

"That's what I thought when I had it prepared." I was hoping that one day the owner would come here and I had it decorated for her.

Big bit his lip, enraged by the skid and Nancy, grateful, exclaimed:

"Very cute. I think it invites us to spend more days in it than we had thought to be here.

Bud, very amused to observe Big's confusion, asked:

"Do you want to see the pastures and cattle now? There is still light and you will be able to judge how it is.

"Well. We will finish the visit.

Bud yelled at Fred, who was gone, as well as Rosa, and ordered:

"Fred, take the boys to the pastures." The gentlemen want to see that.

Fred shot out with the pawns and Big, followed by his daughter and Raft, who looked like a banshee floating around them, headed for the pasture.

The rancher verified that a new thorn fence had been laid, that the cattle had increased in quantity, and that their quality was excellent, and he also noted that the pasture had been expanded with the new land purchased by Bud.

Feigning ignorance, he asked:

"Have you acquired permission to put livestock on other people's pastures?

"No, Mr. Big, those pastures belong to Miss Nancy's ranch."

"How? Have they been given them away?

"Almost. The acquisition was not bad. Those five thousand"odd dollars that you sent me as the balance of our first account have worked miracles.

Big took the hit, saying:

"We'll talk about that later."

Passing through the new sheds he discovered, through the open door, the precious white stallion that Bud had reserved for himself and, staring at him, exclaimed:

"You have a lovely horse, Bud, also on account of that five thousand"odd dollars?"

"Also. Am I not telling you that I have performed miracles with them?

Nancy, captivated by the horse, approached him lovingly caressing him and Bud, with tremors in his voice, said:

"Miss Nancy, that horse belongs to you and you can dispose of it whenever you like." I've been training it for you and I was just waiting for the chance to give it to you.

Nancy hesitated and finally replied:

"Thanks, Bud, save that for when the time comes to settle all the accounts."

They returned to the ranch. Big impatiently warned:

"I'd like us to talk a little business." I think we all need it.

"I am at your disposal.

"Well, for me, you can start whenever you want."

"Excuse me, but I only deal with the interested parties." I can do it with you or your daughter or both, but no one else.

"Are you saying it for Mr. Raft?" If the Lord is as if he were from home!

"Very good, because when the house belongs to you definitively, and it will be as soon as we settle accounts, give it to him if he pleases, and for my part there will be no inconvenience. In the meantime, we will deal with this matter ourselves.

"Well well. Nancy, I think you come a little tired and you will like to rest. Go to the room that they have gallantly prepared for you and let Rosa help you get ready for dinner. As for you, Mr. Raft, you can choose a room and proceed to clean up. You know you are at home.

"Thank you very much, but I'd rather go horseback riding while you go about your business." When I return, we will definitely fix mine.

"Well; as you like!

Nancy went out and met Rosa, who was waiting for him in the corridor, while Raft, a little nervous, unable to define his true situation, went down to the patio, crossed the fence, mounted his horse and trotted to digest the moment. solemn that he lived, because he was in the grip of the greatest anxiety and could not make a decision that would clarify it.

His heart warned him that he was caught by the teeth of a trap from which he could not get rid of, but in any case he had a clear attitude in which he would not give up. He would pay off the debt he owed to Bud, and after God arranged what was most opportune.

CHAPTER XII

HOW A MAN REACTS

They were alone in the office Bud and Big, and then the first placed the accounting books on the board and pointing to them, said:

"Mr. Big, here are all my debts, but since you are in my debt, I expect you to deposit on the table the amount of the previous balance." Then ask me what you think is pertinent.

"Is it essential that I deposit that amount in advance? Is not my word enough to pay it off if it is fair?

"It might be enough, if you had been dignified with me." It is not enough, when you have treated me worse than the last and most despicable of your pawns.

"How have you treated me? What accounts have you given me of your actions and your business? You knew you were dealing in something that was not yours.

"But what I was as interested in as you." What would have become of the ranch if I had not had the ingenuity to acquire money and pay the laborers, expand the pasture land, acquire more cattle, renovate this ruined house and secure its credit?

"I don't doubt that he did it that way, but how did he do it and why didn't he give me a timely account?"

"Because he treated me like an inept and like a servant and I am none of that." I will be poor, because I have squandered my personal fortune, but I have the ingenuity to raise a new one if I put my mind to it.

"I'm not convinced by you, Bud." Give me the accounts later. I'll see if you're right.

"I won't give them to you without first receiving the money."

"I'm sorry, but I can't agree." It would be to return to the subject of your first letter. I repeat that if it is justice, I will pay what I owe.

Exalted, Bud got to his feet, slapped the books, knocking them to the ground, and yelled:

"He is not going to give anything, because I give him everything! I leave him a ranch that is worth twice what it was worth when I took care of him; I leave him twice as much ground as the one he had when I came; I leave you a worthy team and not a crew of cattle rustlers; I leave it paid to him until the day and I leave him more cattle than I found here. I also leave you my seven"month salary, which I give to you so that you can make the wedding gift to your daughter when you marry that fool you have brought in your company, if not before I nail you against the fence for an idiot. I have a fate and it is fulfilled. I was born with the "Colt" in hand and with it I will live until I fall with my boots on, but I will never live under the control of anyone, even if the one who wants it is the father of the only woman I have loved in the world.

Bud pushed the table violently and headed for the door, intending to leave. Big tried to restrain him, but he brusquely rejected him and when he opened it violently, he stopped confused when he discovered in vain the silhouette of Nancy blocking his path.

"Wait a minute, Bud," she said briskly. Would you like to grant me the grace of a few minutes of conversation?

Bud hesitated, but with a violent effort replied:

"You are a woman and I cannot deny a woman anything." You will tell me what you want from me.

"Just reminding him of the conversation we had one night on the patio at Daddy's ranch." He remembers?

Bud, with a lump in his throat, muttered:

"Yes! We were talking about wishing for the stars ... of impossible loves ... of a few more things on the subject.

"Indeed. There was also talk of walls that prevent jumping to take what is most desired. I think I was the one who told you that if you were a brave and risky man to jump those walls ... Have you done it?

Bud stared at her in anguish. In Nancy's eyes a strange fire burned, something great and sublime that was like the promise and the invitation of that night, and, without being able to contain himself, blinded by the splendid vision of her, guessing all that her soul hid and that still He hadn't had time to understand, he put out his arms convulsively, exclaiming:

"Not! I haven't jumped it, damn my soul! But I'm going to jump it now even if I crash in the fall!

And holding her like that night, he kissed her again in front of Big, who burst out laughing.

Bud released Nancy and, turning against him, yelled:

"What are you laughing at?

"What fun I've had at your expense, Bud." I have been continually spurring you on without your noticing and you have played my game without knowing it. Day by day,

I have been informed of how much you were doing here to earn what you most longed for in the world; but I did not think it was appropriate to run my hand over his back praising him, in case he believed it and fainted on the way. There are trails that you cannot rest in the middle of them, because you run the risk of slipping backwards and losing your way. That is why I was prodding him from behind and I did not want to stop until the last moment.

"And what is the last moment for you? Bud asked.

"Because it says?

"Because of that puppet that was brought in as an escort." If your purpose was to put an end to this charade, what was the hindrance?

"That is the last hindrance you have to remove, Bud." Sorry, but there is no other solution. It is a boil that came out a long time ago and that there has been no way to eliminate.

Nancy angrily rose to say:

"That's not right, Dad." All you have to do is fire him.

"No, daughter, Laurence is one of those who are convinced only by fists." I told you and you know it. He has stubbornly come here for you to witness his defeat for the second time and he must be pleased.

Bud, hearing him, left the room, at full speed and going down to the patio, shouted:

"Where is that guy who was accompanying Mr. Big?

"He said he was going out for a walk in the valley." I do not think it will take long.

At that moment, Laurence's horse was outlined in the distance and Bud, his heart overflowing with joy, waited for it to arrive.

When Raft landed on the ground and discovered Bud, he gritted his teeth and asked:

"Has the conference ended yet? May I know what my situation is in this house?

"Yes, and I'm going to point it out to you." I have arranged with Mr. Big and his daughter my next marriage to Nancy. This will give you an idea of your position and now, as I know that you have come with the intention of paying off that outstanding debt, I am at your disposal to settle it, but keep in mind that the end will not change at all for you. Winner or loser, Miss Nancy will be my wife.

Raft went thickly pale when he heard him. He realized, albeit late, that he had been being a plaything in the hands of the cunning Big and a dull rage invaded him.

Controlling his anger, he said coldly:

"It's okay, Bud." You win and there is no more to talk about this matter. I have been a fool not understanding that what happened that night in the ranch yard went deeper than I had supposed, but there is no right to make fun of a man as Mr. Big has done. I may not be a good match for your daughter, but I am not a wimp or coward to be taught bravery with fists.

"You defeated me once when, animated by a deaf rage and great hope, I fought with you to defend my love and I know that you will defeat me better today that the triumphs are yours and I am going to fight for an empty cause; but, for Above all, I want to establish that I am a man to resign myself to defeats, but not to avoid them.

He stripped off his jacket and belt, which he threw aside and said:

"Whenever you want, I'm ready to start ..."

Bud felt all his hatred for Raft dying from his virile male trait, and approaching him he replied:

"Listen to me, Laurence." You know I'm not a coward. You also know that I am going to beat you today better than ever, precisely because I fight for everything and you for nothing. But I want to tell you something that I never thought I had to say to you. Today you have become a nice man for me. You have shown me that you have a virile temper and I pay tribute to whole men. It would hurt me to see him walk away from this battered, broken ranch, full of a double resentment that would lead to nothing. Neither in my eyes nor in Nancy's, you will be worthless if you resign yourself and give up this foolish fight that will lead to nothing. You finish showing that you are a man accepting what fate has imposed on you and take me as an example. I had given up everything in your favor, believing that Nancy loved you. I had already given up on killing him despite being the man assigned to have been born with the "Colt" in hand. One day I was convinced that more things are gained with a song and a guitar than with fists or shots, and I had decided to holster the revolver forever. Don't make me think that it shouldn't be like that and that I should wield it foolishly with you, if after fighting you are not satisfied and you keep thinking of a rematch. What we do not solve as human beings, we will not solve like beasts. if after fighting we are not satisfied and keep thinking of a rematch. What we do not solve as human beings, we will not solve like beasts. if after fighting we are not satisfied and keep thinking of a rematch. What we do not solve as human beings, we will not solve like beasts.

Raft remained tense for a moment, as if doubting in the attitude to take. Suddenly, he took two steps, picked up his jacket and belt, put them on, and, jumping on the horse, he crossed the fence saying:

"Bye, Bud, good luck to you!" Tell Nancy that I am leaving like a coward so as not to lose at least her esteem.

“Bye, Raft! Bud yelled. And don't think that. You are not leaving as a coward, but as a real man. Someday you will recognize it that way.

The horse got lost in the dust on the road, and as Bud went into the yard, he ran into Fred, who, very disconsolate, said:

"Well, old fox, you've already solved your lawsuit, but what about me?" How am I going to solve it, if I have no one to fight with to dispute Rosa's love?

"Not? Bud exclaimed wryly. Now you will see as yes!

And before the naive foreman had time to be on his guard, he slammed a direct hit on the chin that left him sprawled on the flagstones in the courtyard.

Then he carried it over his shoulder and, climbing the stairs, went to the room where Rosa was preparing Nancy's clothes.

The girl, seeing him arrive with Fred's inanimate body, gave a little cry and exclaimed in alarm:

"What's that, Mr. Bud? What happened to poor Fred?

"That he's more of an idiot than me, and that's saying enough." I was very sorry because I had no enemy to fight with to dispute your love and I have given myself to give you that pleasure. Tell me if I let you, or throw you into a pond to drown for an idiot.

Rosa, indignant, exclaimed:

"And that's why you had to mistreat him like that? Do you think I need a shit instead of a man? To love him, the face he has is enough. I don't need to be fist"changed.

Bud, smiling, exclaimed:

"Well then, there's no need to rush." In three or four hours you will have him again. As I was determined not to fight with him anymore, I needed to make him bite the ground sometime and I already have.

Suddenly Fred stood up and, looking at him mockingly, said:

"What do you believe that, you piece of ass! Let's see if you think I didn't see the action! What happens is that I wanted to make fun of you, giving you that stupid satisfaction ..., but, in the end, I thank you, because you have saved me from having to do something more difficult and dangerous for me than to fight with you.

"What? You piece of animal!

"Well, I have to testify to this youngster." That was harder for me than fighting twelve outlaws.

Bud, disillusioned that he did not defeat his rude friend by surprise, exclaimed menacingly:

"It's okay; Make fun of it, but don't claim victory. I swear to you that on the wedding day I am going to give you such a beating that they are going to have to take you to church on a stretcher.

"I should see it! Fred exclaimed. And now, please go away, I have to say a few words to this sugar cube. If you are such an idiot that you waste your time, threatening fights instead of singing love songs to your torment, I am not to blame. Get out of here!

And with a superb push, she put him in the hall, slamming the door ...

END